THE RETURN TO BAYMOOR

The Baymoor Saga

Danyae Brewer

For my cousin, Erica "Ladybug" Wicks —
Your light never dimmed, it just rose higher.
Every dream I chase, every story I tell,
carries a piece of your spirit in it.
You were love, laughter, and loyalty all in one.
Rest in paradise, WE did it.

CONTENTS

Title Page

Copyright

Dedication

The Return to Baymoor   1

Chapter One   2

Chapter Two   9

Chapter Three   14

Chapter Four   19

Chapter Five   25

Chapter Six   33

Chapter Seven   37

Chapter Eight   44

Chapter Nine   50

Chapter Ten   57

Chapter Eleven   65

Chapter Twelve   68

Chapter Thirteen   72

Chapter Fourteen   75

Chapter Fifteen   78

Chapter Sixteen   81

Chapter Seventeen —   85

Chapter Eighteen   90

Chapter Nineteen   93

Chapter Twenty   96

Chapter Twenty-One   99

Chapter Twenty-Two   102

Chapter Twenty-Three   104

Chapter Twenty-Four   107

Chapter Twenty-Five   110

Chapter Twenty-Six   112

Chapter Twenty-Seven   115

Chapter Twenty-Eight   117

Chapter Twenty-Nine   119

Chapter Thirty   121

Acknowledgement   123

About The Author   125

THE RETURN TO BAYMOOR

The Baymoor Saga
Written By: Danyae Brewer

CHAPTER ONE

The block didn't sleep; it swayed. At night the prison found a rhythm—low, bass-thick, made from murmurs and metal and the lazy slap of cards on melamine tables. Fluorescents hummed like tired bees. Somewhere a shower head dripped a fat, steady beat. The air tasted like bleach rubbed over sweat and old cologne smuggled in a cap; like noodles softening in hot sink water and mackerel out the pouch; like men who had learned to live in one square of concrete and still make a life.

They said Baymoor had a sound. This block had one too— the pre-dawn hum of men waiting; the mid-day bark of orders; the night-time celebration when a man was set to "touch the gate" in the morning. Release nights were holy in their own sideways way. Even enemies turned human for an hour. Tonight was Damion's night, and the tier had been on a slow boil since count.

From the doorway of his cell, the view was a slice of everything: dayroom tables congregated into islands; plastic bowls steaming with "spread"—ramen cracked open, crunched into crumbs, baptized with hot water, dyed red with crushed chips; summer sausage coins stacked like poker; a squeeze bottle of "cheese" somebody had begged off kitchen crew; a mirror made from tinfoil and faith; a chessboard carved into the table with a magazine staple. Laughter flared and slid across the ceiling. Someone sang off-key. Somewhere dice knocked like knees.

"Dame" A voice pitched high with youth and pride bounced up the tier. "Come eat, big homie. We ain't letting you starve out on yo' last night."

Damion turned his head. Three boys from the Sevens—Lunnie, Peanut, and Jett—stood grinning under the camera like they owned the angle. All under twenty-two, all wearing state greens like hand-me-downs, all with that bright-eyed way of pretending time wasn't real.

"Man, we got a whole care package walkin'," Peanut bragged, lifting a plastic bowl crowned in crushed chips. "We did the deluxe. Hot Cheeto lasagna. Don't play with us."

Jett waved a spoon like a flag. "And we got dessert: honey bun warmed on the light, extra peanut butter. Chef's kiss." Lunnie tucked his chin, bashful even while clowning. "You gotta come down here, D, Table three. We reserved it." Damion looked past them. Men who'd barely spoken to him all year gave a little nod. A few lifted two fingers in salute. Even a CO at the desk pretended not to notice the clump of bodies; some nights were exceptions you didn't try to regulate unless you liked work.

From the lower bunk, the old man grunted like a chair in a church. Deacon Royce swung his legs out and sat up slow, tattoos like river maps running down his forearms—names, dates, an old crown crossed out with a bold X and a small cross drawn above it. He kept a Bible wrapped in brown bag paper, the corners soft from a thousand sermons given without a pulpit.

"Go on," Royce said, voice a warm gravel. "Break bread with 'em. Let the boys love you while it's easy."

Damion checked the envelope under his pillow with an unconscious hand—letters he could recite like Scripture—then slid it back and stepped out. The floor was cool through thin socks. Metal railings felt like winter. They met him with noise the way the city used to, shoulder slaps, jokes, names thrown like confetti. Bones yelled, "Don't come out there lookin' like you 'bout to propose to your P.O., boy!" and the table cackled. Snipe slid a flimsy chair with a flourish like he was pulling it out for a king. Stacks, who owed Damion two soups from a year ago, pressed one into his hand without making eye contact. People remembered things on release night.

He sat. The table caught its breath, tilted toward him. Lunnie pushed the steaming bowl close enough to fog his chin. "We did it right," Peanut said. "Ramen, sausage, pickles, cheese, Doritos,

Fritos, look—scallions." He lifted an onion sprig like a green flag. "Got the garden in this bih."

"Garden from commissary?" Snipe said. "Boy, shut up."

Jett tucked something under Damion's hand—small, bright, cold. When he opened his palm, he was holding a chain braided from gum wrappers and thread, tight as a promise, with a little cross bent from a paperclip hanging at the middle. "You know," Jett said, suddenly shy. "So you be remembering."

"Remembering what?" Bones called, nosy.

"That we ain't all dumb," Jett shot back. "And that you ain't either. Just… you know. You showed us another gear."

They looked at him like boys look at an older brother walking out to a world they still only see through pictures and stories. They teased to hide it, but their eyes told the truth: they were proud of him and terrified for themselves. Damion nodded once, heavy and slow. They ate. The spread was salt and heat and effort—you could taste the care in it, the way hands in a place like this tried to turn crumbs into communion. They talked with their mouths full and their eyes quick—clowning his old shoes, asking what phone he was gonna get ("you can't come out here with no flip, my boy"), fighting over whose number he should memorize. Peanut produced a crumpled kite—names and digits scratched small—and slid it over. "We ain't goin' nowhere," Peanut said. "Well. Literally. But you get the point."

It could've stayed loud like that, and it would've been enough. But release nights had a way of pulling history to your table. A shadow leaned at the edge of the light. Twan, Committee, jaw like a brick, one eye that never quite lined up with the other. Once upon a three-yard stretch, they had tried to knock each other's heads off with locked fists and words sharp enough to draw blood. Tonight Twan held a cigarette rolled tight in thin white paper, smoke curling like a question mark. The CO's eyes slid past and pretended not to see.

Twan tapped the cigarette ash into a paper cup, showed both hands open.

"No smoke," he said, and the table said "word" in a way that meant more than it sounded.

He looked at Damion for a long second. The block hummed around them. In Twan's eyes, a whole movie ran: yard beefs, five-on-fives that ended with two men in the box and three in the infirmary; mapping out corners like you could own space in a place designed to crush it; making alliances over powdered coffee. Then one night—the one that changed everything—COs swarmed Twan in the showers like hornets after he mouthed off to the wrong suit.

Feet and batons and the mean electricity of men who know they can hurt you. Damion had stepped into it like a fool or a leader, dragging Twan out by the elbow and putting his own body in the way, yelling so loud the whole block heard: *"This between y'all and us. It ain't Sevens vs. Riverstone tonight. That war outside. We men in here. Back off."* They'd both caught a week in the hole for it, but something shifted. Guys pulled up after and said, "We ain't crashin' out with each other no more."

A truce grew in the cracks. Fights didn't stop; they changed direction. If there was smoke, it went upward—toward staff, toward rules, toward anything that wasn't a mirror. Twan sucked smoke and let it go slowly. "I wouldn't be here if you ain't do what you did," he said, eyes on the table. "Or I'd be here in a different way. You feel me." He took another drag, then offered the cigarette. Damion didn't smoke anymore—hadn't since his brother died—but he accepted it, held it like a relic, then passed it to Stacks like it meant we done.

Twan's mouth twitched. It could've been a smile. "Lil D," he said, not unkind. "Walk light out there. Ain't nobody gon' clap when you hug the wrong person." He faded back to shadow and went on, and the table exhaled like they'd all been holding their breath through a prayer. They went back to loud—because boys are built to be loud when they're scared—and fed Damion like they could stuff an extra pound of weight on him that would keep him from blowing away in the morning. He ate what he could and pushed the bowl when he couldn't. He hugged Lunnie and tried not to let the boy feel how hard his heart was beating.

Damion stood. He squeezed the chain in his hand until the little cross bit his skin. "I'll carry y'all," he said. He didn't add *and try not to carry what'll drown me* because some truths don't sit right at a party. Back upstairs, the block still swayed. Laughter thinned to chuckles then whispers. A radio hissed through a news station no one was listening to. A domino bone clicked lonely and stopped. In his cell, Deacon Royce had put water on to steam in a bowl to trick the air into forgiving them. "Smelled like you boys found a garden," Royce said, eyes smiling without his mouth. "They tried to feed me til I remember they the ones still hungry," Damion said. Royce patted the mattress with an open hand. "Sit. Let an old fool say a thing." Damion sat. The Bible appeared with the brown paper crackle, but it stayed closed on Royce's knee.

"You let go of that crown in here," Royce said. "I seen you do it, not with a speech, but with your everyday. That's how real faith show up—small, stubborn, and repetitive. But the street don't like widows, son. It'll come knocking like a jealous woman. Clean hand, dirty hand. It'll try to hold you with both." He didn't preach it; he let it settle on the bed between them like a folded shirt.

"I ain't trying to be two men," Damion said, and heard the doubt in his own voice. Royce nodded, like he was agreeing with the part Damion couldn't say. "Then don't walk the fence. Fence'll cut you open right where the heart sits." He tilted his head. "Pray?"

"Later," Damion lied gently.

"Later comes fast," Royce said, not unkind. He slid back, gave the night back to Damion.

He reached under his pillow and pulled the envelope like a magician palming the final card. He chose the letter by feel—creased heavy, smudged in the corner where fingers had found it on bad nights. But he didn't open the paper. He reached behind it and took out the photo.

Serenity looked back at him in the flat yellow light—chocolate skin warm even on cheap print; natural ponytail pulled high and clean, the style he'd always favored because it made her look like movement; brown eyes with that steadying weight, the way she framed you with a look and made noise fall away; wide, juicy lips glossed, framing white teeth that showed only when she meant it; slim and curvy, a body that read "capable" more than "posed." She had been a firecracker as a girl—fast laugh, faster temper—but time and a child taught her laid back. You could still see the spark in the corners. She wore a simple tee and a chain he'd given her right out of high school, the pendant small as a thumbnail.

He looked and the block blurred. The narrator could have told you oxygen got weird in those seconds; that sound took a step back to respect what the eyes were doing. His thumb dragged the glossy edge. *Let me be better when I see you again,* he thought, not as a prayer, not as a promise. Just a line he put out there like a rope he hoped to pull himself along. Outside the cell, footsteps approached and paused. A knuckle tapped iron twice—the signal that meant

respect more than *answer*. A man stood there—Wrecker, older Committee, two long scars down his forearm, a history of saying hell first. He smelled like tobacco and mint. He didn't look inside right away, like he was talking to the hallway more than the cell.

"We good, D," Wrecker said. "All the way good. Been good since that shower night." He dragged on a cigarette, exhaled smoke toward the vent. "If I ain't said thank you, that's my pride. This is me saying it."

He flicked ash into a paper cup and snorted at his own vulnerability. "Go be out there," he muttered. "Don't come back here." He half laughed. "And if you do—it better be as a visitor to talk to the kids about how not to be me." He smirked, embarrassed by his own sermon, and walked without another look. Royce lifted an eyebrow. "Even rocks can cry out," he said. "Or cough," Damion said. They both smiled a small, private smile.

The night thinned. Voices became thread. A CO's keys talked from far off, then quieted. Somebody started humming a church song and forgot the second verse. Cards clicked one last time and a chair scraped the floor like a sigh.

Damion tucked the photo back safe. He laid the wrapper-chain across his knuckles and watched the little cross glint with every breath. He didn't smoke, but he could still taste smoke—release night smoke, the kind that wasn't about addiction but about ritual. He stretched on the top bunk, hands folded under his head, and stared at the ceiling until the paint made shapes: a map of a city he knew by feel; a crown drawn in negative space; a cross hidden in the angles if you tilted your mind right.

"Revelation say something about lukewarm," Royce said to the dark, voice a thin blanket. "You know the line."

"I do," Damion said. He didn't repeat it. He let it live between them, present and working.

The block exhaled. The steam stopped hissing. The bowl on the sink cooled. The small heat of bodies settled into bunks. Time tucked its chin and watched them in return.

Damion's right hand slid to the mattress where a pistol used to be, once upon an outside. He left it there, empty, and let the emptiness mean something. On a tier where hours usually dragged like shackles, this one glided. He didn't sleep. He waited. He listened for keys that hadn't jingled yet. For a door that would sigh open like old lungs. For shoes that would walk him down, and a gate that would change the temperature of the air on his face.

He waited for morning to knock.

CHAPTER TWO

Before the light changed color, before the vents warmed, before the first radio on the CO desk found its volume, the block held its breath.

Damion was already sitting up when the keys started whispering down the tier. Night had thinned to a gray sheet laid over everything. Men were awake in the way men get when they know a threshold is near: not talking yet, but listening with their whole bodies. You could feel eyes in a place like this. He folded his blanket in even quarters, smoothing the burn mark with his palm. He stacked his state clothes—blues worn a shade lighter at the knees, T-shirt gone soft with a hundred wash cycles—into a square on the bunk like he was building a small, neat memory.

He opened the envelope once, touched the edges of the letters without taking them out, then slid Serenity's photo from the back and let it sit in his hand a moment. Chocolate skin glowing even in cheap ink, natural ponytail high and sure, brown eyes that could still everything in him, wide lips the color of evening, white teeth he used to earn. Slim and curvy, soft and capable; a woman who learned to be calm without losing her spark. He looked until the edges of the picture curled from his grip, then tucked it into the inside pocket of the jeans he'd folded last night—release clothes, clean and waiting like a promise he didn't say out loud.

"Rise and shine," a CO said without any shine in it. The keys paused at their door; the clipboard made a small thump against steel. "Dame. You're up." Deacon Royce sat already, both feet flat on the floor, the Bible in his lap with the brown paper cover creased into the shape of a thousand mornings. He didn't offer a sermon.

He lifted his hand, palm out, and Damion met it.

They didn't bow heads so much as let their chins fall the way men do when they're tired and honest. "Father," Royce said, low enough it felt like the prayer could hide in the seams of the room, "walk this man beyond fences. Close doors that ain't his and open the one that is. Keep his heart from splitting. Make his feet pick one road and love it. Amen."

"Amen," Damion said, and found that the word fit his mouth different today—lighter, but sharpened. He stood and dressed: white tee first, settling over his shoulders like a fresh start; jeans, a little stiff from being folded, the fabric rasping his fingers; socks matched for once; shoes clean because somebody on laundry owed Royce a favor. He slid the photo into the inner pocket, the wrapper-chain with its bent paperclip cross into the other. He smoothed his shirt with open hands the way his mother used to and nodded to the room as if it were a person.

The lock popped—metal against metal, a sound he'd be hearing in his blood for years. The door rolled back with that tired, familiar sigh.

The tier noticed but stayed itself. Reverence isn't quiet because it's empty; it's quiet because it's full. Heads leaned out, hands hooked around bars, eyes lowered or lifted depending on what they needed to hide. It wasn't a parade; it was a church aisle.

"Walk light, Dame," Bones whispered from three cells down.

"See your people first," someone else murmured. "Dodge them streets."

Lunnie pressed fingers through the slot and tapped the rhythm they used last night, softer now, like a coded blessing. Peanut lifted two fingers in a V and mouthed, *we here.* Jett held up a folded scrap—a sketch of a skyline and the words We Don't Wanna See You Again—and smiled without showing teeth. Twan was just eyes from the dark—one steady, one wandering—but he nodded like men do when they've buried a hatchet and marked the ground so they can find it later if they need to prove it.

Even Wrecker coughed himself into speech. "Be the man you already practiced," he said, a sentence that sounded like it had

10

been sanded down all night in his throat. Damion took it all in and didn't rush. He walked the rail with his hand low, fingers brushing steel like he was reading braille from the prison itself. Every step kept a count: door... gate... paper... air. His stomach did that hollow flip you get at the top of a ride you ain't sure you should've boarded.

Receiving & Discharge smelled like rubber mats and coffee burned an hour ago. The CO behind the plexiglass wore boredom like armor.

"State I.D.," the man said, sliding a laminated card into a tray. "You lose it, you'll hate yourself."

A property officer in a blue shirt opened a gray bin. "Inventory: one belt—no buckle. One wallet—no cash. Misc photographs—family. Letters, tied. One paperback—religious. One pair shoes. One chain —non-metal." He ticked each with a pen that clicked like a metronome. "Sign here, here, and initial the release of effects line." He pushed a stack of forms that had been filled a thousand times by a thousand hands, all suddenly individual because the pen was in Damion's. Damion read what he needed to and trusted the rest. He signed his name like he meant it to be seen. He initialed boxes that gave him back small pieces of himself.

Another officer—tired, not unkind—reached into a drawer and took out a thin manila envelope. "Gate money," he said, like he didn't want to argue about the amount. "And a transit card if you need it." He slid it under like contraband. "You got a ride?" "Yeah," Damion said, because he believed Marcus as a matter of religion. "Good," the officer said, eyes flicking up enough to be human. "Don't come back."

A counselor with a necktie too short called his DOC number like a hymn. "Conditions of release," he said. "Your PO info's in the packet. Curfew here, employment there, testing here. Questions?"

Damion had a thousand questions none of these papers could answer. He shook his head and signed what was left. The counselor stamped the last page so hard the desk trembled. "Congratulations," he said, with a face that didn't know how to make the word.

They walked him through hallways that had never cared for sunlight. Paint wearing off the corners where carts had kissed it too many times. A bulletin board with a flyer curling up at the edges: REENTRY RESOURCES in blue letters over a list of numbers that might save somebody whose day didn't start with a brother in a parking lot.

At the last inner door, a CO with forearms like pillars took his measure without moving his head. "Baymoor," he said. "Head up." Damion lifted it. The door sighed open. Air changed temperature.

Outside happened all at once. Sound snapped different—the distant teeth of traffic, a gull arguing with another gull over something shiny, wind moving through a patch of scrub grass near the fence, not air-conditioning but air. Smell came next: damp concrete still holding last night's cool, a thread of exhaust, the salt that lived at the edge of this coastal town and climbed everything it could reach. Light wasn't just bright; it had weight, the kind that sits on your nose and makes your eyes water and tells you what time it is without clocks.

He didn't rush the first step. Men told stories about the stumble, the superstition of it. He placed his foot on concrete he didn't have to give back and let his knee follow like he was learning a new walk. He didn't look for the parking lot yet. He looked up. The sky didn't look different than it had over the yard, but it felt different because there wasn't fence in it. He tasted it like he'd been promised this flavor as a child and forgot the recipe until now.

Behind him, keys spoke once more and fell quiet. The inner door closed with that tired breath he knew by heart, and for a second it sounded like a goodbye that might actually stick.

He checked himself by touch. Photo where it should be. Chain where it should be. Letters pressed flat under the weight of his shirt. He slid two fingers into the inside pocket and felt Serenity's smile in cardboard and ink. He didn't pull it out. He wanted the outside to meet him before he reintroduced the past to it.

"Baymoor!" a voice called from somewhere beyond the glare,

bright and close as laughter.

He didn't turn yet. He let the name hang, taste it, remember that a city said it different than a prison did. The reverent hush from the tier had followed him this far and now thinned into distance. His chest felt hollow and full at the same time—the strange math of freedom: subtraction and overflow in one breath.

He took the next step. Beyond the low chain-link out front, he could see the outline of road, a blue car idling, heat waves lifting off the hood like ghosts deciding whether to stay. He could feel the question the day was asking. It didn't sound like a judge or a threat. It sounded like a fork in a path you've already walked both ways in your head.

He breathed, slow and counted. In for four. Hold for four. Out for four. Deacon Royce had taught him that as much as scripture.

"Head up," he heard again, though the CO was gone now and the voice came from inside.

He lifted it and stepped toward the gate, sunlight laying a warm hand on the back of his neck like it owned him and was willing to share.

He didn't smile. Not yet. He let the moment be its own thing: sweet at the edges, sharp in the middle, heavy everywhere. Bittersweet, like a truth you accept before you understand it. And beneath it all, the hum of Baymoor—waiting, teeth hidden, eyes on him. He crossed the last painted line on the concrete, and the world widened.

CHAPTER THREE

The lot outside the prison looked like every lot outside every prison: cracked pavement, weeds fighting through lines of oil stains, a chain-link fence humming against the wind. One car waited, hood faded, but clean like someone still cared.

Marcus leaned against it, one hand in his pocket, the other shading his eyes from the early sun. Same broad shoulders, same easy posture that had carried him through every fight since they were teenagers. He spotted Damion walking out and stood straighter, grinning wide. "Boy, you got skinnier," Marcus said, shaking his head. "I was expecting a gladiator. Nigga look like he been fasting."

Damion smirked and pulled him into a hug, the kind that was half embrace, half test of strength. "Don't worry about me. Worry if your girl been feeding you too good." Marcus laughed, clapped him on the back. For a second, it was like no years had passed, like prison was just a nightmare they both woke up from. They broke apart, and Marcus searched his face, eyes soft. "You good?"

Damion looked back at the looming walls, the gray stone still spitting shadows even in daylight. His chest tightened. "Get me the fuck away from here." Marcus didn't need more than that. He popped the driver's side door open and slid in. Damion climbed in passenger, the seat stiff under him but smelling like freedom. Westview slid past the windows like a ghost town. Boarded-up houses, corner boys posted too early, a mother yanking her son by the wrist on the way to school. Damion watched it all in silence. Marcus filled the quiet.

"You missed a lot," Marcus said. "Prices gone up crazy, gas

damn near five dollars. Catherine Price still running the city in the shadows, but Reggie Wallace giving her hell with this mayor thing. Nolans making noise, too. Buying people. Caldwell family flipping like pancakes." Damion half-listened, half-remembered. Baymoor had always been a city with too many crowns and too many hands.

Marcus glanced at him. "Look, I got space at the shop. Chair's yours if you want it. It ain't the streets, but it's steady. Good money. Keeps your name ringing in the right way." Damion nodded once, words still caught somewhere in his throat. His eyes stayed on the window. He saw kids with bookbags walking past murals of men who never made it past twenty-five. He saw a girl jump double-dutch in the street, rope slapping pavement like gunshots. He saw Baymoor watching him, whispering. "You listening?" Marcus asked. "Yeah," Damion said. "I hear you."

Marcus took a left, then a right, pulling deeper into the Bricks. "One more stop. Gotta pick up your old car." Damion looked at him sideways. "You really think that bucket still running?" Marcus grinned. "Man, trust me. Just watch."

They turned another corner, and suddenly the street exploded. Music blasted from stacked speakers, bass thumping so deep it rattled the glass. Smoke from grills hung heavy in the air—BBQ ribs, hot dogs, and burgers fighting with the smell of cheap liquor. Kids ran wild, hair beaded and braids flying, shoes squeaking across cracked pavement. Old heads sat on folding chairs, dominoes slamming, dice bouncing against the curb. Women danced near the speakers, hips rolling, laughter carrying over the beat. Bottles passed hand to hand, red cups lifted high.

The whole Bricks was out. And every eye turned to Damion. "Welcome home, Baymoor!" someone shouted. The crowd roared, voices overlapping, hands reaching to clap him, shoulders bumping his. He stepped out of the car and the love hit him like a wave—faces grinning, voices chanting his name.

Marcus clapped his shoulder. "Surprise."

The crowd parted without anyone saying to. At the center stood Serenity. Her chocolate skin caught the sunset like it was painted on her. Hair pulled up in that high natural ponytail Damion had always loved—it made her look both fierce and soft. Brown eyes fixed on him, heavy, steady, unreadable. Full lips pressed together, then parted just enough to breathe. Slim waist, curvy hips, simple sundress that didn't need anything extra. She hadn't dressed up for him. She didn't have to.

At her leg clung a boy. Darius. Wide-eyed, cheeks full, hands gripping her dress like it was the only thing keeping him steady. Shy, but curious, peeking at Damion from behind her thigh, hiding, peeking again. Damion froze. The noise around him dimmed. His pulse in his ears got louder than the music. Serenity held his gaze and didn't move. Marcus leaned in, whispering. "Go ahead." Damion's legs felt heavy, but they carried him forward. He stopped in front of them.   Serenity spoke first, voice steady. "Darius… this is Damion." The boy peeked again. Eyes big, like he was trying to figure out if this man was real. Damion crouched, knees cracking, hands shaking more than he wanted. "Hey, lil man." His voice came soft, lower than usual. "I'm… I'm Damion." Darius buried his face in Serenity's leg, then peeked again. A smile tugged at the corner of his mouth, small but there.

Damion swallowed, heat stinging behind his eyes. He didn't push. He just stayed crouched, looking at him, letting the moment breathe.

The crowd circled back in with other faces.

Jessica—Marcus's wife—stepped up, arms wide, smile bright. "Look at you. Home at last." She hugged Damion tight, smelling like she had been baking and perfume at once, grounding him. "We missed you, brother."

Behind her, Kamari—Serenity's best friend—watched. Loud voice, sharp laugh, hair laid, hoop earrings catching light. She grinned but her eyes scanned him, protective over Serenity even in her smile. Then Andre came forward—Damion's cousin. Taller now, thicker, with a beard filling his jaw. He didn't hesitate. He pulled Damion in hard, chest to chest. "Cuzzo. Ain't no welcome needed. You home." His voice cracked with it. They slapped backs until it hurt, until it felt right again.

For a moment, Damion let himself believe. Music, laughter, ribs smoking, dice rolling, kids chasing each other. His name in the air like it belonged. But Baymoor don't let joy breathe too long. Sirens cut through the bass. Red and blue lights washed the crowd. Music sputtered and died. People froze mid-laugh, mid-step, mid-breath.

Three cruisers rolled up slow. Doors opened. Uniforms poured out. At the front, **Chief Grayson** stepped down like he owned the block. White shirt, badge gleaming, smirk already in place. "Well, well," Grayson said, loud enough for everyone to hear. His eyes locked on Damion like he'd been waiting all day. "Day one out and already throwing a parade? Baymoor don't waste no time, huh?"

The crowd rumbled. Someone shouted, "Man, we just celebrating! Ain't no crime in eating a plate!" Grayson's smirk widened. "Looks like gang activity to me." Shouts rose. "Fuck outta here!" "This the Bricks—we family!" A line of cops pushed forward, shoving at shoulders, barking orders. Marcus stepped in front of Damion, hands raised. "We good! It's just a party, man. Chill!" Jessica pulled kids back. Women snatched cups out of teens' hands. Dice scattered under boots.

One of the younger Sevens, Lil Mace, stepped forward, jaw tight. "We ain't doing shit wrong!" Grayson's eyes found him. "Perfect." He pointed. "Arrest him." Two cops grabbed Lil Mace. He fought back, yelling, "Get off me!" The crowd surged. Hands grabbed, voices screamed.

"Leave him alone!"

"He a kid!"

"You can't do that!"

The cops slammed him against a cruiser, cuffed him hard. Lil Mace's face pressed to metal, blood on his lip. Damion stood still. His chest burned, but he didn't move. He just stared at Grayson. Cold. A slow smirk curled at his mouth, evil and patient. Royce's words rang in his head: *Fence-walkers fall. Don't walk the fence.* Grayson noticed. He leaned closer, speaking over the noise, eyes locked on Damion. "See you soon, Damion."

The crowd roared, cops pushed, people scattered. Grills flipped, music cords yanked, kids crying as parents pulled them inside.

Damion didn't blink. He watched Grayson smirk, then watched the sunset smear blood-red across the Bricks.

CHAPTER FOUR

The next morning, Damion dressed in what Marcus had left folded in a bag — white tee, jeans dark enough to pretend they were new, socks that matched, sneakers that had only walked home once. He slid Serenity's photo into the inside pocket and the wrapper-chain into the other. He looked at the room key on the dresser and left it there; he already knew he wouldn't sleep here again.

Outside, Baymoor had put on its morning. Vendors rolled up metal gates; a man with a bucket splashed water across the sidewalk like baptism; a woman in scrubs walked fast, braid swinging like a metronome. Buses sighed at corners and he let one pass. He wanted the walk to the next stop. Wanted to feel the city under his shoes, hear the pigeons argue on power lines, pass the mural of a boy with angel wings whose name no one said loud anymore.

At the bus stop, the bench burned through his jeans. A city flyer fluttered against the glass: JOB FAIR — REENTRY FRIENDLY in letters that meant well. A kid on a bike slowed, stared, then popped a wheelie as tribute. Traffic pushed and pulled past.

A car eased to the curb and idled. Faded blue Crown Vic, hubcap missing, passenger window stuck a third of the way down. "Baymoor?" the driver leaned over, hand out the window. Barely twenty-one, if that. Face fresh, neck tattoo still pink around the edges. New blood. "Hop in, big homie." Damion eyed him. "You are?" The kid smiled like it hurt. "Rio. From the Bricks. I run with your folks." He tapped the dash. A little seven marker hung from the mirror — a wooden bead painted blue, clipped to a shoe string. "I seen you last night. You family."

Damion's jaw worked. He looked at the bus, then at the car, then at the bus again. Royce's voice said pick a road. But a ride is a ride, and the bus was two stops away. He pulled the door. It stuck. Rio shoved it open with a shoulder. "Door got attitude," he said. "Like my babymomma."

Damion slid in. Vinyl seat cracked, smelling like Black Ice air freshener and french fries.

"Where to?" Rio asked, pulling off smooth.

"Crown District," Damion said. "Marcus's shop." Rio nodded, eyes skating mirrors and corners like a boy taught to live. "You shook the block last night. Old heads still outside this morning talkin' about how the air smelled different 'cause you back." Damion smirked without smiling. "Air smell like ribs and trouble." "Facts," Rio said, grinning. "Grayson a ho for coming like that."

Damion watched storefronts change outside — pawn shop to smoothie bar to pawn shop again, the city's rhythm. "He won't be the last one." Rio drummed his fingers on the wheel, then said it like a confession. "Lil Mace good? They saying they booked him at Central."

"He a kid," Damion said. "That's why they grabbed him." Rio nodded, jaw tight. "We got him."

The car turned under a canopy of oaks that made the street feel cooler than it was. Crown District, with its brick sidewalks, law offices, and churches that had good parking. The barbershop lived on a corner with a bright blue door and a window that promised *Fades. Tapers. Line-Ups. Community.*

Rio parked crooked and hopped out first, like he was opening a door to a throne room. "Go ahead, big homie," he said, sweeping an arm. Then he lowered his voice. "And uh, if you ever need anything... I ain't the toughest, but I'm on go."

Damion put a hand on his shoulder. Squeezed once. "Be smart before you be on go." Rio nodded like he was writing it down inside his head. He climbed back in, the Crown Vic coughing smoke as it pulled away, tail light blinking a secret message. Inside the shop, a bell rang, and Baymoor opened its mouth. Clippers sang into brown skin. Laughter crowded the air with good-natured violence. A debate about last night's game tripped over an argument about if raisin potato salad was a crime. Aftershave cut through it all like a sermon. Posters on the wall showed cuts that had ruled different summers; a faded Polaroid near the register caught a frozen moment of Marcus with a high-top fade that should've been illegal.

"Look what the cat dragged in," a barber named Tone said, grinning wide, apron smudged with talc. "Baymoor himself."
Marcus looked up from a chair, blade poised at a teenager's temple. His eyes lit. "First day at the office," he said, and flicked his wrist — a crisp line appearing like he'd drawn it with a ruler. "Grab that broom and act like you never left."
Damion took the broom with a little bow, played along. He swept hair in half-moons, listening to the city talk where it still trusted itself. A kid got roasted for asking for waves when his hair was stubborn.

An old head told a story about a championship in '98 that grew more glorious with each retelling. Somebody in the back sold bootleg cologne with a flourish like he was dealing art. Damion laughed. It came out rusty at first, then easier. The shop held him. For a minute, he could pretend the world fit. The door chimed. Reggie Wallace walked in wearing a suit that made the AC feel warmer. Not a flashy one — good cut, good cloth, tie muted. He shook hands like a man raised by women who taught him to respect a room. "Marcus," Reggie said, smiling. "Your fade's still tax deductible." Marcus snorted. "Only thing deducting around here is that hairline, Reggie." They dapped. Reggie turned to Damion and let his smile stay but softened his eyes. "Damion," he said. "Welcome home." Damion nodded. "Appreciate you."

Reggie's gaze flicked across the room and back like he was checking exits while keeping a conversation. "I heard about last night," he said, voice dropping a shade. "Grayson's working a narrative. Don't let him write you into it."
He reached into his jacket and slid a card across the counter. Clean font. Number that rang. "If you need anything — legal, jobs, pressure off your neck — you call me. Politics ain't church, but I

ain't playin' pastor, either. I mean that."

Damion took it. Reggie's eyes held him a second. Genuine there, and calculation riding shotgun, but not steering. "Appreciate you," Damion said again, and meant both parts. Reggie touched the brim of a hat he wasn't wearing. "Be safe," he said, and left the bell to ring in his place.

The door chimed again before the ring finished fading. Serenity walked in with Darius.

The shop shifted, the way a room does when a story walks into it. Men straightened. Tone lowered the music by instinct. Marcus's grin went wide as he shook his cape loose from the teenager and clapped the chair. "Prince Darius," Marcus said. "Come get handsome." Darius climbed in careful, eyes big as the mirror. He sat up straight when Marcus tucked the cape around him, proud to be part of a ritual as old as fatherhood.

Serenity stood close, hand on the chair's back, fingers tapping a silent rhythm. She caught Damion's eyes. The look carried last night and the years before it. An invitation and a warning. He nodded toward the door. "Step outside a sec?" he asked. She glanced at Darius, then at Kamari's text lighting up her lockscreen, then back at Marcus. "You good?" "I got him," Marcus said. "Gon' send him back with a crown."

Outside, the day had decided to be beautiful. Sun slid along the brick of the Crown District buildings like it was trying to find the perfect color. Traffic moved polite. A church bell somewhere far laid a chime over everything like a blessing you could almost hear. They stood side by side on the sidewalk, not touching. Close enough to feel each other's heat. Not close enough to make a promise.

"You look..." Damion started, then decided to be honest. "Beautiful." She rolled her eyes like he'd said something he couldn't help. The corner of her mouth tugged anyway. "You look... like you slept in a hotel with a loud air conditioner."

He laughed, real. "You ain't wrong." Silence sat with them for a beat, but it wasn't empty. It was two cups filling. "How you been, Ne?" he asked.   Serenity glanced at the sky like the answer was written up there. "Working. Momming. Not exploding." Her eyes moved back to him. Softer. "Missing stuff I forgot I could miss." He nodded, soaking it like a dry sponge. "Last night," he said. "Before the mess… it felt like a movie I didn't know the ending to." She breathed in. "Darius ain't stopped talking about you since." Her smile was a small sunrise. "And about the fair. He been begging me for a week. Rides, funnel cake, the works."

"Let me take y'all," Damion said, too fast and exactly right. "Let me go." The softness in her face pulled back a little, like a tide remembering the moon. "You know Tyreek," she said, and let the name sit there, an object they both could see. "He ain't gonna like you around Darius like that. Not in public. Hurts his pride."

Damion's jaw flickered. "I ain't asking him."

"And I ain't trying to raise drama at a place with kids," she said, gentle but steel underneath. "Pride gets loud. Ego gets reckless. You know that." He did. He'd invented some of those rules, once. He nodded. "How we do it then?" She looked through the shop window at Darius under the ring of Marcus's hands. "Andre's taking Darius," she said. "He said he'd ride with him, keep eyes up. Kamari riding with me. If you want to meet us there… that's a way."

It wasn't the way he wanted. It was the way that fit today."Alright," he said. Then, softer: "I wanna be near him. Not to spook him. Just… I don't want to miss the smile when he wins something." Serenity watched him say it, watched his face rearrange around the word want. She nodded once. The tide crept back toward shore. "Come by tonight," she said, like she'd already decided before she asked. "After the fair. I'll cook."

The word did something to him he didn't show. "What you making?"She smirked. "Don't be picky. First round is spaghetti. You can earn baked chicken later." He laughed again, and it felt like a part of his chest that had been locked up got a window. Inside, Marcus lifted the hand mirror and spun Darius toward the light. A line lay across the boy's forehead sharp enough to cut paper. Darius smiled at himself in a way that made the room brighter; he looked grown and still very much a child, which is the only magic that matters.

They went back in. Serenity kissed Darius's cheek through the cape. Damion stood at the edge and let himself be the wall he needed to be, not a shadow. Reggie's card peeked from Damion's pocket like a reminder: the world had already made appointments for him. Politics had knocked without knocking. Streets had sent a car. Love had said spaghetti like a prayer.

Marcus popped the cape, hair snowing to the floor. "You the freshest kid in Crown," he declared.

Darius slid off the chair, feeling his own head like a king. He looked at Damion then, held his eyes a second longer than yesterday, and said, ridiculously proud, "I look like Marcus." "Now that's an insult," Damion said, grinning. The shop laughed. Plans moved without a calendar. Andre texted: *On my way*. Kamari: *We good*. Serenity checked the time. The day leaned forward like a man about to stand.

Damion slipped the card deeper into his pocket and palmed the wrapper-chain until the little cross bit his skin. He didn't ask for a sign. He'd already gotten three.

Outside, the sky was the color of new hope and old warning.

CHAPTER FIVE

Serenity's place held morning like a song she knew all the words to. Sunlight leaned through the kitchen blinds in careful stripes, dust motes floating like lazy confetti. A candle on the counter read Clean Cotton but smelled more like home than laundry. Darius's sneakers were by the door, one on its side like it had run out of gas. Cartoon chatter from the TV in the front room played too loud and then not at all because he'd wandered off to find another toy.

Kamari was posted at the kitchen island with a makeup bag exploded like a flower—lashes in a little coffin, gloss standing at attention, a brush that looked like it cost too much money for how fast she swung it. She watched Serenity pull her ponytail tight in the microwave reflection and shook her head. "Okay, ma'am," Kamari sang, "ponytail sitting high like you finna file taxes on a man." Serenity rolled her eyes but couldn't kill the smile creeping up. "It's a ponytail, Mari." "It's *the* ponytail," Kamari corrected, snapping her compact shut. "The Damion ponytail. I know it when I see it."

Serenity pressed a palm across the top of her hair and smoothed the edges with two fingers. "I'ma take it *slow*."
"Mm." Kamari sipped from a mason jar like it was tea and gossip both. "And I only get one lash per eye. Girl, please. You took a *half day* off feelings, not a sabbatical." They both laughed, the kind that drops their shoulders and puts years back where they belong. Darius thundered through, cape made from a towel, yelling "Zoom!", then bounced into the living room again as if joy had a route and he'd memorized it.

Serenity leaned on the counter, chin in hand. "He asked about Damion first thing. Didn't even brush teeth yet. Just 'Is Damion coming to the fair with us? Is Damion tall enough for the rides?' All morning." Kamari softened. "See? Kids know what's what. He read that man like a book at story time." Serenity's eyes lowered. "I'm not rushing anything." "You're trying not to *call it*, that's what you doing," Kamari said. "And I love you for the effort. But also, girl, you glowing like a house with good wiring." Serenity scratched a thumbnail along the counter's fake marble seam. "I told him I'd cook tonight."

Kamari grinned like a trap snapping shut. "Oh, we cooking-cooking. What you making? Don't say boxed mac." "Pasta," Serenity said. "Quick. Garlic butter, maybe shrimp if I grab some. Salad if I'm feeling righteous. Garlic bread 'cause I ain't." "Okay, Chef Ponytail," Kamari said. "Add a little red pepper flake so he know you got layers." Serenity smirked, then cleared her throat. "Can you babysit? After we get back?" Kamari opened her mouth, then covered it with dramatic hands. "Ahhh, see, I was gonna let Andre babysit *me* tonight." She blinked sweetly. "Ask **Jessica**. She love playing auntie and she owe you from the time I watched her cousin's cousin's twins. I'm still tired."

Serenity pointed a finger. "You ain't watched them kids but forty minutes." "And I aged six years," Kamari said. "Do the math." They both laughed again, lighter than the hour before. Darius slid back into the kitchen in socks, crashed into Serenity's hip, and hugged her without saying anything. She bent to kiss his scalp. "Ready for the fair, lil man?" Kamari asked. He nodded so hard the towel cape flew sideways. "I want lemonade and a turkey leg and the big bear." "You want *everything*," Serenity said. "Everything," he agreed solemnly. "Go get your shoes," she said, and he rocketed away like obedience was a race he intended to win. Kamari looked back at Serenity when the boy was gone, voice dipping. "You happy?" Serenity's smile got quiet. "I could be." "That's all I needed," Kamari said, zipping the makeup bag like a final answer.

"Let's go see about it."

The Baymoor Fair sat across three dusty blocks of the old riverfront like it had never left—an empire of squeaks and lights. Banners flapped on poles, colors shouting over the wind. The Ferris wheel threw slow circles into a bright sky, cabin windows catching sun like coins. Somewhere close, a man with a fryer made funnel cakes disappear under snowstorms of sugar. Turkey legs smoked in a row like fists. A teenage DJ under a tent begged speakers to be brave.

By the time Serenity, Kamari, and Darius threaded through the entrance, Andre had texted *we at the midway*, and Marcus had sent a selfie of him making a face while Jessica laughed behind him, a turkey leg trying to upstage them both. Damion was there in the photo too, smile small but present, eyes busy like always. They spotted each other near the ring toss. The world narrowed and then widened again.

"Ma!" Darius squealed, pointing without need. "They here!" He ran ahead and then stalled, suddenly shy, slowing to a walk as he approached Damion. Damion crouched like the earth had instructions, palms out like a peace offering. "Hey, lil man," he said. "You made it."
Darius looked at Serenity for a yes that had already been given, then stepped close enough to bump knuckles. "We gon' get the big bear."
"It's written," Damion said, dead serious, and Darius beamed.

Kamari threw Andre a look and got swooped into a hug that lifted her off her sandals. "Put me down," she laughed, slapping his shoulder. "You heavy-handed love language."
"Only for you," Andre said, grinning like he'd built the sun. Jessica wrapped Serenity in arms that said family. "You cute," she declared. "Ponytail doing the Lord's work." Serenity laughed into her shoulder. "Girl, shut up." Marcus clapped Damion's back. "You ready to be a kid today?"
"I'm on probation from adulthood," Damion said. "Darius is my P.O." "Say less," Marcus said.

They started with lemonade in long cups, condensation slicking fingers, then went hunting grease: corn dogs, popcorn, and nachos with cheese that didn't apologize. Darius bit a turkey leg like it owed him money, chewing with his whole face. Kamari narrated like a sportscaster.

"Look at him conducting," she said. "This is art."

Then came the rides, Darius dragging the whole crew like a small general with good intentions.

"Everybody gotta get on at least one," he decreed, taking attendance with a straw. "Even you, Auntie Jess." Jessica gasped. "Even me?!"

"Yes," he said, the law.

Bumper cars first—Marcus and Andre turned into ten-year-olds in under three seconds, ramming each other like insurance had never been invented. Kamari shriek-laughed every time Andre spun out and then swore on everything holy that she only screamed because "this car steering is a lie." Jessica bumped Marcus and then kissed him on the cheek at a red light, which made a teenager in the next car groan "eww."

The Tilt-A-Whirl caught up Damion and Darius together. The boy's hands clamped to the bar, eyes wide, scream ready, and then joy found him mid-spin and he laughed so loud other cars looked over to borrow it. Damion kept his arm a whisper above Darius's chest—close enough to catch, far enough to let the kid fly.

On the Ferris wheel, they split—Marcus and Jessica to one cab, Andre and Kamari to another. Damion and Serenity shared a bench, Darius in the middle like the axis of something finally making sense. The wheel carried them up into a view of Baymoor that made the river look like a blade laid flat. Wind tugged at Serenity's ponytail. The city hushed for them. "Thank you for coming," she said, watching the water. Damion didn't say *for you, twice over*. He said, "Wouldn't be anywhere else." Darius leaned into him without looking. Damion swallowed a knot and let his palm rest against the boy's shoulder like a vow.

Back on the ground, game booths lined up like challenges.

Damion stopped at the water-gun race, paid in crumpled bills, and narrowed his eyes like aim was a prayer. The bell rang, streams shot, and a row of plastic horses started their journey. He found a rhythm. The bell dinged. A light flashed over his spot. "Winner!" the carny announced, not unhappy to lose to a man who looked like he needed a win.

Damion picked a small blue bear and handed it to Serenity without fanfare. It wasn't big. It wasn't nothing. She took it like he'd given her a sentence she'd been waiting to hear. Her eyes said *I see you* and then *be careful* and then *thank you* in one blink. The group saw it. Kamari stuck her tongue out to hide a grin. Marcus elbowed Jessica. Andre raised eyebrows like *look at God*. But nobody said a thing. They let it be theirs.

Damion played again and won a bigger bear that almost matched Darius. The kid yelled like a stadium. Marcus, not to be outdone, knocked down three milk bottles and won a panda for Jessica after missing twice on purpose to make it fun.

Andre fumbled two throws and then banked a third, swaggering over to hand a flamingo to Kamari. "Why a flamingo?" she asked, delighted. "Long legs," Andre said. "Thematically appropriate." "You're stupid," she said, kissing his cheek.

They ate funnel cake dusted heavy enough to make them cough and laugh, fingers sticky, faces sugared. The day dimmed itself toward gold. The fair changed color; lights woke up in lines. Jessica reached into her bag as they paused by the lemonade stand and pressed a key fob into Damion's palm. "By the way. Hotel?"
He nodded once, shoulders rising with the admission. "One night."

"Not again," she said, simple. "My cousin's place—an Airbnb —empty all week. Code's in your text. Stay there. It ain't fancy, but it's clean and safe. I already told her you're family." He didn't do pride. Not with family. "Thank you." "Don't thank me," she said. "Just don't disappear."

They started toward the exit in a loose cluster, stuffed animals riding on shoulders, Darius in the middle bouncing between hands like a spark.

That's when they saw them coming in. Calvin first—pressed shirt, cool face, a gravity that made space behave. Tyreek beside him, jaw set, eyes scanning, Tiffany and Brittany trailing in step like an entourage and a test. The air tightened the way it does just before glass breaks. Tyreek's eyes found Serenity and burned without warming. His voice didn't need to be loud to cut. "Oh, that's why you ain't pick up," he said, stepping close enough to be a problem. "Had to bring my son up here with this lame-ass nigga?"

Heads turned. People love a show they ain't paid for.

Serenity didn't break stride. She smiled, tired and sharp. "Boy, go back to your lil' girlfriend." She tipped her chin toward Tiffany without looking. Tiffany popped off like a firecracker. "Lil who? You tired, sweetheart. You real tired. Dragging that man around like a clearance sale—" "Chill," Calvin said without urgency, eyes on Marcus and Andre as if doing math. Cold watcher energy. Not a peacemaker. An accountant of risk.

Tyreek reached out, fingers opening, grabbing for Serenity's arm like he'd forgotten who he was and where they were.

Damion's body moved before the rest of him did. He didn't square up. He didn't talk. He turned, stepped into the angle, and put one clean right on the side of Tyreek's jaw. A single lick. *Thunk*. Quick enough to make the word sudden feel slow. Tyreek's legs emptied. He crumpled, arms catching air, mouth open like he'd been asked a question too hard to answer.

Chaos poured in. Tiffany screeched, pointing, cussing loud enough to make a gospel tent cross itself. Brittany pulled her back by the wrist, cussing at her cussing. A circle formed like it always does when trouble draws chalk no one can see. Calvin took a step and stopped. Andre had already moved, stance wide, hands open, eyes without smile. Marcus stood a half-step forward of Damion, chin up, barber's hands ready for a different kind of line work.

Calvin's eyes did the math and closed the book. He didn't reach for Tyreek. He didn't reach for anything. "Let's go," Serenity said, voice steady, hand on Darius's shoulder. The boy's eyes were wide, lip tremble tucked inside bravely. "We leaving."

They did. Not in a run. In an exit. Damion didn't look back. His knuckles buzzed like they had memorized a frequency he didn't plan to play again. Behind them, Tiffany's voice kept trying to be a siren. The fair swallowed it in lights and rides and a song that had already moved on to another chorus.

Jessica's cousin's Airbnb sat over a small storefront a few blocks off the main drag—two rooms, floors that creaked honest, a couch that had done its time and still had kindness left. The kitchen held mismatched plates that didn't mind each other. The bathroom had a plant determined to live. Serenity kicked off her shoes, dropped her purse, and tied on an apron like that made it official. "You like garlic?" she asked, already spinning a pan, flame snapping blue.

"Love it," Damion said, setting the bears on the couch. The little blue one leaned against the arm; the big one took up a cushion like rent was due. She boiled water, salted it the way her mother taught her—*til it tastes like the sea*—and slid in pasta like a promise kept. Garlic butter turned the kitchen into a halo. Shrimp hit the pan and curled into commas. She chopped parsley with a speed that said she'd done this in four different apartments and a house she didn't live in anymore. A bagged salad turned righteous, garlic bread crisped, and in fifteen minutes the room smelled like a truce.

They ate at the small table, knees near, shoulders close, laughter soft. They didn't rehash the punch; they let it sit where it landed. They talked about little things that made the day big: Darius conquering the Tilt-A-Whirl, Kamari screaming on rides she picked, Jessica threatening to report the funnel cake for being too good.

After dishes—two plates, two forks, a pan—Serenity found a movie on some free app with too many commercials and settled onto the couch. Damion sat beside her. She leaned into him first. He exhaled like he'd been holding it since morning and let his arm fold around her shoulders. They watched the story try to be a story. Outside, a car passed with music low enough to live with. Inside, they made a quiet that wasn't empty.

When the final commercial ended and the credits tried to matter, Serenity clicked the TV dark. The room held their breathing like it had been waiting all day to do that job.

"You safe here," she said, simple.

He kissed her forehead. "I am right now."

She tucked herself under his arm and let sleep climb her like a vine. He stayed awake a little longer, eyes on the ceiling, hand on the wrapper-chain in his pocket, thinking about fences and roads and how a kitchen can smell like a decision. When sleep found him, it didn't ask questions.

CHAPTER SIX

The Bricks at night had its own kind of peace. Not quiet —never that—but peace in the way familiar sounds stack into comfort: the buzz of a streetlight fighting for its life, a dog barking two blocks over, the hiss of somebody's grill still smoldering, laughter leaking from an open window where the TV was too loud. The park at the edge of the projects wasn't much—two busted swings, a slide tagged with paint that had been there longer than some of the kids, a crooked bench—but it was space. Space to breathe, space to talk, space to remember you weren't inside a box anymore.

Damion leaned back on the bench, legs stretched, a red cup in his hand. Marcus sat at the other end, rolling a blunt with the patience of a man braiding hair, while Andre stood nearby, propped against his car like he owned the night. Two women from the Bricks—Sevens affiliates—hovered close, smoking and laughing between themselves, sipping cheap liquor. The kind of women who weren't gang members, but were gang family —sisters, cousins, friends. "Boy," Marcus said, licking the blunt closed. "I still ain't over that *one-punch KO* at the fair." Andre laughed, head tilting back. "Man, Tyreek folded like a beach chair. Nigga hit the ground before his pride did."

The women cackled, one slapping her thigh. "Whole fair seen it too. Tiffany still mad 'cause she had to help his dumb ass up." Damion smirked, sipping slow. "Y'all extra. It was one lick. Ain't no highlight reel." "Nah, nigga," Marcus said, lighting the blunt, smoke curling into the night. "It was perfect. Legendary. You shoulda heard the crowd. Boy, people still talkin'. You hurt his pride worse than his jaw."

Andre shook his head, eyes sharp even with the laughter. "And pride don't heal. He coming back for that. Bet that."

"Let him," Marcus said, puffing smoke. "We here. Together. We straight."

Damion let their voices fade into the night's rhythm. He wasn't ignoring them. He just knew truth when he heard it, and Andre was right. Pride was gasoline. Baymoor was full of matches. A car rolled slow up the block, headlights dimmed, engine purring like it didn't want to be noticed. Damion clocked it without moving his head. Marcus exhaled smoke but cut his eyes sideways. Andre shifted off the car, shoulders stiff. "Who dat?" one of the women asked, frowning. The car stopped. Doors cracked. Shadows spilled out—two, three figures, faces half-covered, hands heavy with steel. And in the passenger seat, behind the glass, Tyreek.

His head turned just enough for the streetlight to catch his grin.

"Move!" Andre barked, but the night had already ripped open. Gunfire exploded, shredding silence into rags. *Rat-tat-tat-tat!* Sparks jumped off the swingset, wood splintered from the bench. Bullets punched through Andre's car door, glass snowing the ground. The air filled with the smell of metal and smoke, sharp and choking.

The women screamed and hit the ground. One tried to crawl behind the bench but Damion grabbed her arm and yanked her flat, shielding her with his body, voice low and steady: "Stay down. Don't move."Marcus cussed loud, dragging another woman by the wrist into cover, then peeked up with rage burning his eyes. "Them Riverstone niggas really wildin'!"

Andre ducked behind the car, jaw clenched, watching the shooters fan out. "They aiming for us!"

The gunmen let off another round, heavy and reckless, sparks dancing off the metal poles, bullets chewing through dirt where feet had been seconds before. Then, as fast as it came, the burst ended. Tires screeched. The car swallowed its soldiers and peeled off, fishtailing smoke into the street, gunfire echoing in memory more than air. The park exhaled, broken.

Glass crunched under Andre's boots as he stood, dusting himself off, checking for blood that wasn't there. Marcus straightened slow, face tight, hands shaking even though his voice stayed calm. The women sat up, wide-eyed, hair wild, hands still clutching air like it could protect them. "One of y'all saw it, right?" Marcus said, scanning faces. The thinner woman nodded fast, still breathless. "That was Tyreek. I know his whip. Chrome rims, dent in the back door. That's his shit. He came hisself. Petty-ass." Murmurs went up, voices overlapping: *"Nigga brought it here."* *"They really tried to body y'all."* *"Shit starting again."*

Two younger Sevens came running from down the block, guns in hand, eyes wild. "What's up? Who was it?"
"Committee," Andre growled. "They tried to hit us."
"Then let's slide now!" one of the boys snapped, pacing like a pit on a chain. "We can't let this go. They gon' think we soft!"
"Tonight," the other added, already loading his clip. "We know where they be."
Damion rose slow, brushing glass from his jeans. His face was unreadable, eyes like dark stone. "Not tonight."

The younger one whipped his head. "What you mean not tonight? They just shot at you, Marcus, Dre—" "I said *not tonight,*" Damion cut him off, voice low but final. "That's what they want. Us rushing out blind. Us losing two, three more. That's their play." Marcus stepped forward, voice steady. "Baymoor right. We don't move sloppy. We don't move scared either, but we don't move dumb."
Andre nodded, crossing his arms. "Y'all young. Y'all don't remember the last war. Bodies every week. Mothers burying sons. You want that back?"

The younger Sevens shifted, anger simmering but respect holding them in place. Guns still in hand, but lowered. The women shook their heads, muttering like prophets no one wanted to hear. "It's starting again. You can feel it." Damion looked around the park—bullet holes in the slide, glass glittering under the streetlight, a bench split down the middle. He didn't speak. He didn't have to. The picture said enough.

Inside his chest, the thought he didn't want sat heavy: *If I don't guide this, somebody else will. And they'll guide it straight into hell.*

He stared down the block where the car had vanished, smoke still hanging in the humid air like a warning. His jaw set, his mind running quiet and fast. Marcus broke the silence. "What you thinking, D?" Damion didn't answer. He just watched the night close back over the street, bullet smoke rising like incense.

CHAPTER SEVEN

After hours, the shop felt different—like a church after the congregation leaves. The clippers slept on their hooks, cords curled like tired snakes. The aftershave still hung sweet-sharp in the air, mixing with talc and the faint burn of disinfectant. Blinds were drawn halfway, neon from the liquor store across the street bleeding in through the slats and painting thin blue lines across chairs flipped belly-up on their cushions. The bell over the door was taped so it wouldn't ring. The Crown District had closed its eyes for the night, but the shop was awake.

Marcus slid the deadbolt and turned the sign to CLOSED even though everybody inside already knew. He and Andre moved two chairs to the side and pulled the round table from the back— where the chessboard lived—and set it in the middle like it was a drum. Men came in quiet, palms slapping shoulders, hands gripping hands. OGs took the wall—Uncle Rome with his gray beard and slow blink, Big Walt thick in the shoulders but light in the feet, Nate-O scar over his eyebrow from a decade that never stopped bleeding in his stories. Young Sevens bled into the space— Rio from the Crown Vic, Dez with restless eyes, Kilo playing tough with a nervous jaw. The room balanced itself: youth and history, heat and memory. Damion sat at the table, Marcus leaned behind him on the station, arms folded. Andre stood at the door with a hand on the knob like a doorman at a speakeasy, checking eyes, checking intent.

It had been two days since the park. Two days since the shots chewed metal and wood and didn't find flesh. Two days of whispers in the Bricks, of boys eager to turn whispers into noise.

Kilo didn't wait for ceremony. "We spinning or what?" he said, voice already up a notch. "They came for the heads. They came for y'all. They think we sweet 'cause Baymoor home and wanna play nice. We can't wear that."

"Facts," Dez chimed, pacing in a tight square. "They had Tyreek in the passenger seat like a trophy. He ain't hiding. He flexing. We gotta show we ain't scared."

Uncle Rome's voice cut soft but carried. "Scared ain't the question, little man. Question is: you ready to buy what that move costs?"

Kilo tossed his hands. "I'm ready to pay whatever." He said it like a kid daring a stove.

Big Walt snorted, a sound like furniture shifting. "Everybody ready till the receipt come with names on it." Rio's voice landed somewhere in the middle. "We ain't saying crash out, Unc. We saying we need a call. We ain't got no call right now. We got ten different boys ready to lead ten different packs into a wall." Andre knocked his knuckles on the table twice, a barber's tap for attention. "All that movement without a center? That's how a war starts. And ends ugly."

Marcus lifted his chin. "Last time this block went dumb, we had moms picking out suits they ain't buy for prom. Y'all don't want that rerun. Not 'cause you scared, because you smart." Kilo rolled his neck like a boxer between rounds. "So who calling the plays then? 'Cause Calvin calling his. Committee ain't waiting."

Silence slipped in, not long, but thick. Heads turned like the room had a magnet in one spot and everybody's eyes were iron. They looked at Damion. He didn't jump to fill it. He watched the young ones burn. He watched the OGs hold water. He let the quiet do some of the work.

"You gave it up," Uncle Rome said finally, voice a gravel road. "We respected you for that. But you ain't just a person here. You a position. And positions don't like being empty."

Marcus's gaze slid to him. "We need you in the seat, bro." Andre added, "Not for clout. For order."

Damion rubbed a thumb along the groove in the table where the chessboard edge had worn a notch. He could feel the ghost of a knight, the shape of a move. He tipped his head, still not speaking. The room started to answer itself.
"Vote then," Nate-O said, shrugging on a sigh like a jacket. "Ain't nothing to it but to do it."
He raised his hand. Big Walt followed without a word. Uncle Rome's palm rose like a blessing. Rio's went up quick, then steadier when he saw the elders. Dez's hand climbed like a dare. Kilo held out half a second on instinct, then lifted too, eyes down because he hated that agreement could feel like surrender.

Marcus didn't raise his hand. He just stepped off the station, came around, and stood behind Damion's chair like the back of it was a throne.
Andre didn't raise his either. He posted at the door and watched the whole room raise theirs.
Damion looked around once, slow, counting without counting. Every hand. He didn't smile. He didn't speak. He let his shoulders settle one notch lower, like something heavy had been set there gently. The tape over the bell did its job, but the door still gave a tiny chirp when it opened. Suits don't usually look right in barbershops after hours. Reggie Wallace made it fit by not pretending like he belonged; he stepped in like he was entering someone else's living room and took the temperature before he asked where the thermostat was. "Evening," Reggie said. No smile. Just respect. Marcus lifted his chin. "You heard?" "Everybody heard," Reggie said. He moved toward the table but didn't sit, choosing instead to keep a hand on the chairback like he might need to move fast in either direction. "Committee hit y'all in a public park. Police 'coincidentally' nowhere close. Chief Grayson already on the phone talking about increased patrols in the Bricks for your 'protection'." The word came out like a bone he didn't want to chew. Dez scoffed. "Protection my ass." Reggie nodded.

"My point. I'm not here to give a speech. I'm here because the city is—" He searched for the word, found it. "— susceptible.

One spark and you don't just lose a corner. We lose Baymoor. Catherine Price will march into office on the bodies. Cops will have a blank check. And you—" He looked at Damion and did not blink. "—you will be the headline they cash."

Kilo bristled. "So we sit and sing, councilman? We hug it out?" Reggie didn't bother getting offended. "You do what you want. You're going to anyway. I came to say this: if there's a man in this room who can make strategy out of anger, it's him." He turned his chin toward Damion. "And if there isn't, Grayson gets what he wants without writing a warrant."

Uncle Rome scratched his beard. "Boy speaking like somebody who's seen a calendar or two." Reggie exhaled, a small tired sound. "I'm speaking like somebody who's been to too many funerals and too many ribbon cuttings for programs that don't save the right people." He set a card down on the table, the same clean font, the same number. "Whatever you decide, let me help you do it smart. Legal cover. Eyes in City Hall. Pressure where pressure saves lives instead of exploding 'em." Damion hadn't moved. He looked like a statue cut from patience. Reggie read the room one last time and nodded to Marcus.

The bell chirped. The door clicked. A breath nobody knew they were holding left ten lungs at once. For a second, no one spoke. The liquor store neon blinked a tiny rhythm through the blinds. Outside, a bus sighed. Damion's phone buzzed in his pocket. He didn't move. It buzzed again. He pulled it, screen lighting his face in cool light.

Serenity: *I see y'all from across the street.*

Another beat, then the next: *Please don't do nothing to get yourself sent back. Darius needs you here.*

He stared at the words, the way the second text was the same sentence Royce had prayed, just with names attached. He didn't type. He breathed. He slid the phone back like you put away a picture you're not done looking at.

"You got the vote," Marcus said, not a question.

"Say the word," Rio added, eyes bright and scared and loyal. "We ain't wild dogs," Uncle Rome said. "We soldiers if we're anything. Soldiers need orders."Damion's eyes dragged around the circle, took inventory: scars and eagerness, wisdom and impatience, fear pretending to be anger, love dressed as anger's twin. He laced his fingers, knuckles whitening, then relaxed his hands and let them rest flat on the wood. "We ain't crashing," he said finally, voice even, low enough that men had to quiet their own to hear it. "We ain't making nobody's job easy. Not the Committee's, not Grayson's." He looked at Kilo. "You want to spin? Spin on your discipline. You want to ride? Ride on your mouth—closed. We move when I say move. Not for pride, not for clout. If a move don't save somebody or secure something that matters, it ain't a move— it's noise."

Kilo opened his mouth, then shut it when Big Walt's elbow found his ribs. Damion kept going, not faster, just surer. "We find out where they soft—for real, not in your imaginations. We count who we trust. We cut who we can't. We get the women and the kids a plan before we get bullets a target. Y'all want me back?" He lifted his chin a fraction. "I'm back. But you follow, or you leave. No in-between. Fence-walkers fall."The word hung, a bridge back to a cell where an old man had warned a younger one about the taste of lukewarm. Nobody asked how he knew. The room knew.

Uncle Rome nodded once, the kind of nod men give when they've seen five generations of the same story and this is the only version worth sitting through again. Big Walt rubbed his hands together like a man getting ready to work, not fight. Nate-O closed his eyes and whispered something that might have been a prayer or a curse begging to be reversed.

Dez lifted his chin. "So what's step one?"

Damion glanced at Marcus and Andre—brothers by history and by choice. Marcus met his eyes and gave him that barber-chop nod:

clean it up, make it sharp. Andre's mouth didn't move, but his eyes said I'm here. "Step one," Damion said, "we lock this room. Names only. No 'friends of' sitting in on what ain't theirs." He looked at Kilo till the boy dropped his gaze. "Step two, we check the block for holes: cameras that don't work, lights that don't light, paths the Committee used last time. We fix our house before we go staring at somebody else's. Step three, we find Tyreek's tells. He got 'em. Pride ain't quiet. Somebody in his camp talk even when they ain't talking."

Rio nodded like he'd been waiting for a list to hold onto. "Say less." "And step four," Damion said, tapping the table once, "we get the women what they need. Numbers. Rides. A way to leave if it get hot. If we ain't protecting them, burn this flag now."

"Big step four," Uncle Rome murmured, almost smiling.

Kilo shifted. "And when we—"

Damion's eyes cut over and Kilo corrected mid-sentence. "And if we gotta slide…?"

"Then we slide when it means something," Damion said. "And when we do, it won't be for a photo op. It'll be because Baymoor needed surgery, not a tantrum."

Silence for a heartbeat. Then a ripple of low "mhms," the sound of men agreeing with their throats because their mouths weren't built to admit relief. Marcus clapped once, soft. "Y'all heard him." Hands went to pockets, to chins, to the backs of necks where tension had lived and now had a place to go.

The vote hadn't been the coronation. This was. Not trumpet loud—heavy. The kind of heavy you shoulder because the alternative is watching somebody else drop it on your foot.

Through the slats of the blinds, Damion could see across the street: Serenity's boutique, lights low, the silhouette of her moving inside, folding clothes, straightening what was already straight. She'd sent the text and stayed where she could see them, like a lighthouse that didn't blink. He let his eyes rest there for half a second and then brought them back to the room that would eat him if he forgot to look.

"Alright," he said. He stood, and the room stood with him. "Lock in."

Marcus killed the front lights. Andre slid the deadbolt again. OGs and young bloods drew close to the table. Heads bent. Not to pray —though some of them might've. To plan.

The crown didn't shine. It bit. It settled on Damion's head like a set of rules written in a language that only hurt could teach. He felt the weight dig into his scalp and didn't reach up to touch it. Outside, somewhere near the liquor store, a siren yawned and thought better of it.

In the quiet between the floor's creak and a man's next breath, Baymoor held still—and then kept moving.

CHAPTER EIGHT

Rusty's office sat above a warehouse with no sign, down a street that only GPS and hustlers respected. Inside, the décor was money apologizing for concrete—glass desk, leather chairs, a framed photograph of a ribbon cutting with a mayor who'd since resigned. On the wall, a mounted flatscreen showed Baymoor's river at dusk like the city was trying to seduce its own reflection. Calvin came in crisp: navy suit, no tie, eyes that didn't blink unless they had to. Rusty didn't stand. He just gestured to the chair opposite and pinched the bridge of his nose as if a migraine were trying to write its name behind his eyes.

"Sit, nephew," Rusty said, voice sanded smooth by a thousand negotiations. He wasn't actually Calvin's uncle; in Baymoor titles traveled by respect and history, not blood. Calvin didn't sit. "You called." "I did." Rusty looked up, eyes now sharp. "You're cut off." Silence. The river video kept gliding. "Explain," Calvin said. "You don't need an explanation. You need a thermometer." Rusty thumped the glass desk with two fingers. "You and your Committee been running hot for weeks. Now you brought a drive-by to a park and the talk is Ceasefire Season is canceled 'cause Calvin got his nephew trying to prove he's a wolf."

Calvin's jaw flexed once. "There were no bodies." "Not last night," Rusty said. "But bodies ain't the only problem. Heat is. You feel it?" He pointed toward the street, meaning the news trucks, the cops, the whispers. "Our lines don't carry weight when the whole city staring. Laundering dries up when pastors start preaching with names in their throats. Money hates attention." Calvin finally sat, slow. "You want me to leash Tyreek."

"I want you to lead," Rusty said. "Your nephew loud. Loud is a scent. Cops follow scent. Catherine Price got cameras aiming at the Bricks and Crown both, calling Reggie 'soft on gangs' all over TV, and you handing her the script." He leaned back. "You want product? You want the ports? Cool the block, son. Or find new friends."

Calvin's face didn't move. Inside, a small flame ate through the varnish on his pride. He wasn't a gangster; he'd never claimed that. He was a businessman with a city for a spreadsheet. War was a negative line item. He knew it. Rusty knew it. He also knew Tyreek wasn't built for a crown, only a camera.

"Understood," Calvin said.

Rusty nodded once. "Fix it."

He didn't say *or else*. He didn't need to. The river kept gliding, pretending it wasn't listening.

Two nights later, Westview Baptist opened its doors past curfew. Not for worship— for mercy. It was the most neutral ground Baymoor owned that didn't wear a badge. Downstairs in the fellowship hall—long tables, metal chairs, a Coke machine humming like a tired choir—the air held the memory of potlucks and shut-in baskets. Now it held something sharper.

Reggie Wallace stood near the coffee urn with a stack of notes he wouldn't read. He'd been on TV all week—Catherine Price calling him soft on crime, anchor nodding like gravity. He'd said the right things: "community investment," "targeted enforcement," "faith leaders." The comments online wanted blood. The calls to his office wanted someone arrested, anyone. This meeting was the only kind of answer he trusted.

Damion came in first with Marcus and Andre. The three moved like a sentence with commas—same language, different rhythms. Damion's eyes swept the corners, then the exits, then the ceiling vents. Habit. The church smelled like Pine-Sol and coffee and the old wood of trouble trying to stay repentant.

"You good?" Marcus asked under his breath.

"I will be if this stays what it's supposed to be," Damion said.

45

Andre checked his phone, then raised his chin toward the door. "Guests." Calvin entered with Tyreek half a step behind, two Committee lieutenants lingering near the stairs like punctuation he could take or leave. Calvin's suit was a no-color gray; his face matched. Tyreek wore loud: designer tee, chain arguing with the cross above the snack table. His jaw still remembered the fair. Pride held ice to it and called that healing.

Reggie stepped in the middle. "Appreciate y'all coming," he said. "We're here because Catherine Price already made us into a headline and Grayson can't wait to run it as a script. Baymoor is dry tinder. One more spark—" "Spare the sermon," Tyreek cut in, voice too big for the room. "We ain't scared of headlines."
Calvin didn't look at him. Not yet. He looked at Damion. Damion returned the look and then spoke to the room like he was reading coordinates. "Here's the math. Sevens don't sell drugs. We never did. War brings heat to the only people in this room who profit from the drug trade." He let that hang. "Y'all outnumbered three to one in the city. That's not chest— that's a census. You push a war, you don't just lose bodies. You lose business. Price wins the mayor's seat off your mistakes. Grayson drags half this room in on RICO. Rusty starts taking calls from people who ain't you."

A lieutenants' mouth twitched. Calvin's didn't.
Damion's tone didn't rise. "I control mine. I've kept boys still who can't even sit through a movie. I can keep them still longer if you give me reason. Seven-day cooldown. No drive-bys. No daytime hits. Schools, churches, and homes untouchable. We set a contact chain—one call if anything fouls, not fifteen guns. That's my offer."
For a second it almost felt like the room moved closer to the right answer. Tyreek laughed. Loud, brittle, made for an audience. "You feeling yourself 'cause you caught me slipping at the fair," he said. "You ain't king of nothing. You a has-been with a fresh line-up." Andre took a step before he remembered he wasn't twelve. Marcus's hand found his elbow, a barber stopping a bad cut before

it happened.

Calvin's head turned a degree. "Tyreek," he said, soft warning.

Tyreek kept going, volume up. "We the Committee. We spend money. We pay people. We run this. And you—" he jabbed a finger across the table at Calvin now, the room tilting from bold to blasphemy, "—you acting like yo' scary ass hiding behind your money." The lieutenants went still like dogs in a thunderstorm. Reggie's pen stopped moving. Marcus exhaled once through his nose. Andre smiled, which in his mouth did not mean joy. Calvin didn't raise a hand. He raised the temperature—by not moving at all. He turned his eyes on his nephew with a calm that rewrote the air. "You done?" Tyreek's mouth opened. No words came. The church's Coke machine hummed louder. "Good," Calvin said, and turned away as if the boy had emptied his usefulness onto the floor.

Tyreek looked around for rescue—found none. His pride flailed for oxygen. He kicked his chair back so it yelped against tile. "Y'all can sit here and hold hands," he spat. "I'm out."

He left like he wanted the door to slam and couldn't figure out how to make a soft-close church door behave. His footsteps went up the stairwell and into Westview, where pride could still pretend it was a plan. Silence held court. Reggie didn't fill it with words. He set his pen down and looked at Calvin. "That's one choice," he said. "You got another one sitting at this table." Calvin watched the stairs a beat longer, then let them be stairs. He breathed, once. When he looked back at Damion, something had cooled and clarified.

"You're right about the math," he said. "And about Rusty." No one flinched at the name; everyone knew it without having to agree it existed. "Price wants a war so she can ride in with a flag. Grayson wants a war so he can ride in with a warrant. I want... quiet. Quiet is profitable." Damion's face didn't change, but the room felt it: a door opening a crack. Calvin continued, voice clean as a ledger. "Seven days. No drive-bys. No daytime. No churches, schools, or homes. If one of yours steps wrong, you call me before somebody dies." He flicked his eyes at Andre, at Marcus, then back to Damion. "And you keep your boys off my distribution. You don't touch my lines, I don't touch your people."

Andre leaned forward, elbows on table. "And families stay out of it. No girlfriends, no kids, no mamas used as message boards." His tone wasn't negotiable.

Calvin inclined his head. "Agreed." Reggie finally let some air into his voice. "Then we got a truce." He swallowed the word like it had thorns. "I'll handle the public cover—'community leaders collaborating to restore peace,' blah blah. Price will hate it. Good. Grayson will try to poke it. Don't give him a hole big enough to fit a press release." Marcus looked at Damion, then at the far wall where a cross hung above a bulletin board crowded with potluck sign-up sheets. "We can live with seven days. If it buys twenty more."

Damion nodded once. He didn't offer his hand. He offered his eyes. Calvin matched them, then gave a small, precise nod—the kind a man gives when he chooses survival over pride and calls it leadership.

Chairs scraped. Papers shuffled. The lieutenants relaxed their jaws a degree. The Coke machine went back to humming like it had a choir to cover. Upstairs, the sanctuary lights were off; a sliver of stained glass still threw a blood-red line across the hallway like the church was reminding them where they were. At the door, Reggie paused, looking between the two men who could break or build his campaign with a text. "Thank you," he said, and meant it the way a man drowning thanks a board for floating.

Calvin left with his two like a quiet storm that had decided the city could live another day. The stairwell swallowed them. Outside, Westview held its breath and didn't know why.

Marcus pressed his palm to the back of Damion's shoulder. "Good call."

Andre finally let his grin show. "Boy almost melted in public calling his own uncle soft. That's a family problem now."

Damion didn't smile. He glanced at the frosted basement window—light from streetlamps smearing in lines—then at his phone. No text. He almost typed one and didn't. He heard Deacon Royce in the back of his head: *You pick a road and love it.* He pictured Serenity closing her boutique upstairs of Crown District, flipping the sign that kept her safe and open at the same time. He pictured Darius asleep, mouth open, one hand clutching the blue bear.

"Seven days," Damion said, half to the room, half to whatever was listening above the vents. "Make 'em count."

Reggie put a hand to his tie like it was suddenly too tight. "I'll run interference with Price's people. And I'll get ahead of Grayson—if that's possible." He looked at Damion. "Don't give him your shadow to step on."

"We won't," Marcus said.

Andre checked the stairwell one last time. Clear. He flipped the light off over the long tables and the fellowship hall fell to a softer dark.

They climbed to the side door together, shoes whispering on linoleum. Outside, Westview's night pressed in, curious and suspicious. The church shut behind them with a soft click that felt like a delicate promise trying to hold.

Tense in Tyreek's wind, hopeful in Calvin's wake. A fragile peace, real enough to save lives if nobody breathed too hard.

CHAPTER NINE

Main Street wore its Sunday best on a weekday. Crown District shops rolled up their gates like eyelids waking to a miracle; church ladies in sneakers, old heads in Kangols, little kids with beads and barrettes, OGs and YNs from both sides —the Sevens and the Committee—all folding into one long river of people. The signs were homemade and perfect in their imperfections: STOP THE VIOLENCE, PUT THE GUNS DOWN, OUR KIDS LIVE HERE. A pickup crept along the curb with speakers bungee-corded to the bed, Marvin Gaye asking what's going on over a drum loop, and somebody's cousin on the mic calling, "Baymoor, let's walk."

Up front, Damion, Marcus, Andre, Calvin, and Reggie moved shoulder to shoulder—five men who didn't belong in the same sentence yesterday.

Behind them, at a pace that meant *together but not reckless*, came the women and the families: Serenity, Jessica, Kamari, and even Tiffany and Brittany, flanked by aunties, cousins, and girls who'd grown up peeking out of windows at sirens. Darius held Serenity's hand and the little blue bear by one ear, eyes soaking everything like a sponge.

"You know Tyreek too stubborn to show face," Tiffany said, not loud enough to start anything, just enough to be understood. She wore peace like an outfit that fit but wasn't her usual sneakers, no shine, shoulders squared. Brittany smirked, not disagreeing. "He allergic to doing right in public."

Serenity huffed a small laugh. "I appreciate y'all coming."

"We tired of the bullshit too," Brittany said, simple. Tiffany nodded once, the kind that means *don't make me say it twice*. It wasn't friendship. It was something braver—solidarity without softness.

The march moved.

OGs kept tempo with old knees, heads high, faces carved into patience. YNs walked tight and proud, hoodies up, eyes everywhere and nowhere, repeating the chant like a drumline: "No more funerals! No more funerals!" A barber from two blocks over pushed a stroller with one hand and held a sign with the other. A grandmother prayed under her breath as she walked, each step a bead on a rosary. A teenager live-streamed with a cracked phone and a caption that read: HISTORY.

People leaned out of bodegas and boutiques. A cook in a greasy apron stood in a doorway holding a spatula like a flag. Cars honked in rhythm. For three blocks, Baymoor felt like it could re-name itself. "Look at this," Marcus murmured, voice half prayer, half proof. Andre bumped his shoulder, grinning. "They can't say we didn't try." Reggie's tie loosened itself a notch, sweat beading at his temples, but his smile stayed sober. "Keep it slow. Keep it human." Damion felt the hum through the soles of his shoes—the tremor of hope trying to build a spine. He didn't chant. He held the line. Calvin walked in his own math, eyes clicking through cost and benefit, but even he couldn't hide the way his chest lifted when a kid slapped his palm and said, "Mister Calvin, stop the violence!"

The river rounded a bend—and hit a dam.

Blue lights washed the block in police. Cruisers flared sideways across the lanes. A line of riot gear—helmets, batons, shields—stretched from curb to curb like a wall the city paid for and prayed it wouldn't have to live behind. At the center, Chief Grayson stood without a helmet, white shirt pressed, jaw flexed around a smile that liked itself too much. The speakers cut. The crowd's sound thinned, confusion fluttering like a thousand small wings. Reggie stepped forward, hands open, voice pitched to carry.

"This is a permitted march on a public street," he said. "We are exercising—"

"This is an unlawful assembly," Grayson's voice boomed, some lieutenant gifting him a bullhorn like a crown. "Disperse immediately."

A wave of No! rolled the crowd, more hurt than angry. The OGs didn't flinch. The YNs set their jaws in place. Calvin moved a half-step forward, chin up. "We're peaceful. You see families. You see children." His voice wanted to climb and didn't. "Cal," Damion said, eyes still on Grayson. "Chill." Reggie joined, hands still open like calm was a thing you could display. "Chief, we spoke to your office. Your officers are here to ensure safety, not end a march. You can walk with us or you can—"
Grayson's smile kissed the bullhorn. "Damion Carter and Calvin Price—you are under arrest for inciting a riot."

A sound rose from the river that wasn't words. It was disbelief scraped raw. "Hold up," Marcus said, already pulling his phone, already planting his feet. Andre's shoulders tightened, but his eyes slid to the women and the kids like a compass pointing home. The first pair of officers hit the front line fast, hands out, voices hard: "Hands behind your back!" Shields bumped bodies that had come here to be gentle. Another line moved left, creeping toward the families. A baton tapped a shin like a warning no one asked for.

Calvin's elbow jerked—instinct or pride—and a cop grabbed it like a lever. "Get off me," Calvin barked, bucking once. "Cal," Damion said again, low, the word a rope he threw. "Calm." Reggie stepped between them and a baton. "Record everything," he shouted to the crowd, voice cutting clean. "Do not intervene physically, but record. Badges, names, faces—keep your cameras up!" "Step back!" an officer snarled, shoving him. Reggie didn't. "I'm an elected official!" he said, and they took his wrists like the title was a toy. "I said record—don't you put those phones—" The cuffs ate his sentence. "Back up! Back up!" Grayson's bullhorn sang, even as officers pressed forward. He didn't look at the women yet. He wanted his close-up with the men.

Two cops closed on Damion. He didn't run. He didn't talk.

He planted his feet, turned his head just enough to find Serenity and Darius in the crowd, eyes wide, mouths small. "I'm okay," he told her, voice calm like a Sunday morning. "Get him out of here." "Damion—" Serenity's voice broke on the second syllable. "I'm okay," he repeated, eyes steady, that same almost-smile he'd given Grayson once before, the kind that said *you can't eat my peace.* "Go."

Serenity scooped Darius and the bear in one motion, throat tight, Jessica already at her shoulder, Kamari on the other side. "This way, baby," Jessica said to Darius. "Look at Auntie," Kamari coaxed, but the boy looked back anyway, eyes filling, bear dragging. "Daddy!" he cried without asking permission from vocabulary, and the word landed like a brick on two hearts. Hands took Calvin's wrists. He resisted once more on reflex, then Reggie's *calmer heads* echoed in his skull and he stilled, face pale with a fury he kept behind his teeth. Grayson leaned in just enough to be heard over his own theater.

"This what leadership looks like?" he purred. "Headlines and handcuffs."

Damion didn't answer. Grayson hated that. He pivoted to Reggie, now cuffed, shirt untucked, hair out of place.

"Thought you were mayor material," Grayson said. "Turns out you're just another gang mouthpiece."

Reggie breathed slow through his nose like a man refusing to gift oxygen to a fire. "Camera's on," he said to nobody and everybody. "Keep filming." And the batons swung. It started near the middle of the march—an officer shoving an OG for not moving fast enough. An auntie screamed. A shield kissed a teenager's shoulder for standing tall. A cop barked at a mother to get her stroller off the street, then knocked the wheel sideways with his stick when she didn't move fast enough. The stroller caught and righted. The baby cried because the world had raised its voice. People stumbled, pressed, scattered. Riot lines advanced like a bad tide. "Move!" Marcus shouted, grabbing Tiffany's elbow with gentleness big hands barely get credit for. "This way. Keep Darius between y'all."

"I got him," Tiffany said, already flanking Serenity like the universe had given her one good job. "Hold tight, lil man. We ain't letting no boogeyman get you."

Brittany took the other side, head on a swivel. "Phones up," she told the women behind her. "Tuck the kids in close. Don't run, just move."

Andre stepped into the edge where confusion turns into stampede. He planted and parted people with open hands and a calm voice. "Slow—slow—this way—eyes up—breathe." Someone swung a baton at his forearm and he took it with a grunt, grabbed the stick with his other hand for a second because all his muscles remembered how to win, then let it go, remembering seven days and a truce signed in the basement of a church. He backed up, pulling bodies with him, clearing a path for the women and the kids.

Behind them, OGs linked arms—the old universal code—forming a seam in the crowd so the wave broke on them and not on toddlers. A young Committee head who had never in his life walked alongside a Seven now found himself cheek-to-cheek with one, both grimacing, both holding the line against the same storm.

Grayson lingered over the front line, basking in his own ugly handiwork. He tilted the bullhorn, his voice syrup and vinegar. "Baymoor can thank your leaders for this," he announced for the cameras. "Rioters dressed as peacemakers."

Cameras didn't blink. Phones didn't waver. Somebody shouted badge numbers. Somebody else shouted scripture.

The cuffs clicked on Damion—metal cold, wrists already marked by a thousand lives he almost lived. He kept his eyes on Serenity's back as she moved Darius out of the crush, braid whipping like a metronome for survival. Darius looked back again, tears streaking his cheeks, the bear's blue face streaked with street. "I'm okay," Damion said one more time, and the boy tried to believe him.

The squad doors yawned open like mouths that learned hunger from policy. Calvin ducked in first, jaw set, eyes black with thought. Damion followed, the officer's hand on his head like this was a courtesy. Reggie went last, still telling strangers to keep their cameras up, still naming streets like he was mapping a story a jury might actually hear. The doors slammed. The sirens chose a key and screamed.

By the time Marcus and Andre steered the last cluster of women and kids onto a side street, the march had become a cautionary tale. Dust hung where chants had been. A sign lay cracked in half on the asphalt: OUR KIDS LIVE— the last word torn by a boot. Serenity crouched to pull Darius into her, both arms wrapping him until his breath remembered itself. Jessica pressed a bottle of water into her hand that she didn't drink. Kamari stood watch, eyes hard, mouth soft, the same way you look at a house you love when the wind's trying to peel it. "Ma," Darius hiccuped, still peeking around for what he'd lost. "They taking him?" "They taking him to jail," Serenity said because she refused to lie to him when the world already did. "And he's gonna be okay." She said it again until the words learned their lines. Tiffany wiped at her eye like dust had picked today to act up. Brittany swallowed hard and didn't say what she had seen last summer when it was different men and the same uniforms. Marcus rubbed Andre's bruised forearm without looking down at it, then looked up at the skyline like it could answer questions.

Night fell fully and Baymoor turned on its living room TVs. News anchors smiled with their mouths while their eyes practiced sympathy. "Gang leaders arrested for inciting riot at so-called peace march," the crawl said, polite as a knife. A clip rolled: Calvin shouting one frame, Damion being cuffed the next, Reggie in mid-sentence as a hand took his arm. The anchors shook their heads at the violence like it had arrived from outer space. But the phone videos told a different story in the city's group chats and private pages: women shielding children, OGs linking arms, a baton cracking a sign that didn't even have wood thick enough to make a point. Reggie's voice slewed across screens—Record everything —then cut off as the cuffs found him. One clip caught Grayson up close, the taunt in his mouth, the glint in his eyes that wasn't duty. Comments stacked: THIS WAS PEACEFUL. WE SAW THEM. #BaymoorAgainstBrutality. Someone posted a still of Darius crying with the caption OUR KIDS SAW and you could feel the city's heart pinch. In living rooms across the Bricks and Riverstone, OGs stared at the soundless news and heard past wars in their bones. YNs scrolled with thumbs that twitched like triggers and tried to think with muscles made to sprint. Mothers put kids to bed and told them stories about mornings that always come, even when night tries to stay. Politicians measured donations and decided which lie to wear tomorrow.

On Main Street, a single paper plate slid along the curb, catching blue light and red, blue and red, until a breeze finally ushered it home.

Baymoor had asked for peace. The system answered with war. And the cameras, for once, did not blink.

CHAPTER TEN

Holding felt like a lie the building told itself: fluorescent lights pretending to be daylight, metal benches pretending to be furniture, cinderblock pretending to be clean. The air tasted like bleach and old breath. A camera in the corner blinked a red dot that felt like a mosquito you couldn't swat. They packed the cells uneven—Sevens shoulder-to-shoulder in one, Committee in the next, overflow mixed where a deputy got lazy or generous, depending on how you read men. OGs sat with backs to the wall, slow blinks counting time; YNs paced tight circles, shoes squeaking, hands fluttering like birds caught indoors. Voices snapped at first.

"Man, they came for us like we threw the first punch—" "Whole city saw them cops swing, but we the ones cuffed—" "On my mama, if I had one more second—"
"Shut that down," an OG said without raising his voice, and the YN shut it down.

In the Committee cell, Calvin stood near the bars like he thought he could negotiate with steel. His suit jacket was gone, shirt open at the collar, calm face with anger living behind the eyes like a caged thing. "Listen up," he said, turning to his YNs who were doing laps with their mouths. "This is on me. I should've kept my hands at my side and my voice on low. Pride ain't policy. I forgot that for a second and gave them the angle." He let it land. "My fault."

A murmur ran around the cell—surprise first, then relief. OGs nodded because real men naming it out loud always re-arranges a room. Across the aisle, Damion sat on the edge of the bench, elbows on knees, hands open. He looked like rest could find him in a place designed to chase it off. "We ain't break a law," he said, steady, not loud. The men leaned closer to hear, which made the words heavier. "We marched. Cameras got all of it. Women, kids, banners, us up front. They threw the first swing. Let 'em. I ain't in here embarrassed. I'm in here documented."

A Seven across from him—Rio—let his shoulders drop, breath shaking out like a dog after rain. "So we won?"

Damion's mouth tugged. "We didn't lose."

One of the Committee boys across the way laughed once. "That what winning feel like? Smell like mop water and bad decisions."

"Sometimes," an OG answered, "winning start out looking like patience." The edges softened. Someone brought up the game—last night's box score—like the stats could mop up blood the news had tried to spill across their names. A debate sparked over Top Five MCs, quickly devolved into Top Five Verses You Screamed in Middle School, had older men rolling eyes but nodding when a line hit right.

Two Sevens and a Committee head realized they both grew up off the same block before the project buildings where built. Andre tilted his head and started tapping out a beat on the bench; Marcus shook his head, smiling in spite of himself, then added a bassline with his knuckles. Men clapped on two and four because the city had taught them better.

In a corner cell, Reggie sat with his tie in his pocket and a phone nobody was supposed to have in his palm. It had arrived through a chain of favors that ended with a deputy who owed a choir director. He stared at the screen, thumb hovering over a name he'd saved under Auntie Pat even though Patricia had never baked him a pie. She was a state representative who'd once told him, "Call me when it's righteous and risky."

He called. "Patricia Lawson," the voice answered, clipped, tired, professional. The thrum of a car in motion underlined her words. "Representative Lawson, it's Reggie Wallace."

A pause, then a softer inhale. "You're calling from a jail." "Yes, ma'am. Happily." "That's not a sentence I hear often."

He stood without meaning to, shouldering a wall. "We marched. Permitted. Kids, strollers, pastors. Chief Grayson blocked the street, called it unlawful, and ordered arrests like it was a parade for his ego. They cuffed men in front of their sons. They shoved elders. I told folks to record it, so they cuffed me, too. The video's already moving."
"What exact charge?"
"Inciting a riot. For walking with banners and singing 'Lean on Me.'"

A breath that might've been a quiet laugh and a curse. "And who's in with you?"

"Damion Carter. Calvin Price. OGs from the Sevens and the Committee. Too many YNs whose mamas think the system is a haunted house and they just got dragged inside."
"And you're asking for...?"

He exhaled the thing he'd been saving. "A release order. No bond. You know as well as I do you can light the phone tree when you want to. The AG's office doesn't want Baymoor trending for police abuse two weeks before committee meetings on grants. And Catherine Price has already called me soft on crime on three stations; if this sticks, she'll run that all the way to November. Or —" he let it hang— "you can be on every camera tonight saying you protected the First Amendment when a bad cop tried to step on it."

"You running for mayor or for the pulpit, Reggie?"
"I'm running for children to watch their fathers walk home after a march, not get stuffed in a cruiser." Silence that sounded like thought.

"Grayson's got friends," she said finally. "He'll say you escalated."
"Cameras got him escalating. And if the state doesn't look cleaner than the city on this, people will remember at the ballot box. You know Baymoor's counties swing when they believe."

Another pause. The car hummed. "You bargaining with my conscience and my math, Mr. Wallace." "I'm bargaining with time. Every hour our men sit, the story rots." A rustle, a pen on paper.

"I'll make the calls. Sheriff, AG liaison, Chief Judge. I can't promise how fast the processing moves, but the orders will come. And Reggie—"

"Yes, ma'am?"

"Walk out like you won't apologize for it."

"I wasn't planning to."

Reggie ended the call. The phone disappeared the way it had arrived. He looked up and met Damion's eyes through bars and air. "Help is coming," he said simply.

"Bond?" Calvin asked from the next cell, voice carefully bored.

"No bond," Reggie said. "Just out."

A beat of disbelief. Then the sound in the room changed. Not loud. Warm. Palms slapping palms. Men exhaling like a choir finding the same note. An OG who never smiled with his eyes. A YN wiped at a laugh like it might embarrass him.

Calvin tilted his head at Reggie. "You could be processed first. The cameras want you out there hugging grandmothers."

"I'll wait," Reggie said, sitting back down and crossing his legs like the bench was leather. "We walk out together, or we sing in here until they run out of paper."

Damion's mouth tugged. "Sing what?"

"Boosie," Andre said, tapping the rhythm again. Men snapped fingers, hummed, then found the words. "Without that badge..." The sound filled cinderblock like water finding its level. A deputy walking past paused, frowned, kept moving.

Footsteps that thought they mattered came heavier than the hymn. Grayson passed the cells like a parade marshal, clipboard in hand, eyes licking faces as if he might taste defeat if he got close enough. "Ain't a concert," he said dryly. "Enjoy the accommodations while you can afford them." He stopped at Calvin's bars, then Damion's. "Y'all wanted headlines. You got 'em." Calvin stared through him like the man had put on glass instead of clothes. Damion just let the smallest smile visit his face and leave.

Grayson leaned a fraction closer to Reggie's cell. "How's the campaign, Councilman? Figure out how to spin obstruction into 'leadership' yet?" Reggie didn't look up. "Keep walking, Chief. You don't want to be in the background of my release photo." The chief's jaw twitched. He took a step back, turned away—and froze at the sound rising outside. Chanting. Not one voice. Many. A tide pushing against stone. The men inside went quiet together, as if rehearsed. They moved to the front of their cells, heads tilted, listening like they'd heard their own names from far away.

"Free them all!" The chant rolled up the stairwell and down the hall. "Free them all!"
Grayson's eyes narrowed. He motioned to a deputy. "What's the situation outside?"
"Growing," the deputy said, not quite hiding the surprise. "Started with families from the Bricks and Riverstone. Now I'm seeing church vans from Westview, teachers from Pine Gate, folks with signs. Media too."

"Who's leading?"
"Looks like the women," the deputy said, as if that violated a policy. "Serenity Carter. Jessica. Kamari. Those two from the Committee side—Tiffany and Brittany. They got kids up front. Men on the sides keeping the line." Grayson's mouth went thin. "Hold the line inside. No releases without my say-so."

He turned to go—and stopped again when a clerk hustled up with a stack of papers. "Orders from the state," she said, breathless.   "Judge signed. Release without bond. All non-felony march-related detentions."

Grayson read the top page, jaw set. He looked like a man forced to eat something good for him. "Processing will take time," he said to the hall in general, as if anyone had asked. "Nobody goes anywhere until the forms are done."
Reggie rose and smoothed his shirt. "We'll be right here," he said, and sat back down like he had all night and the next day too.

The chant outside shifted, adding claps, building a spine. "Let them go! Let them go!" Children's voices climbed on top of it, bright and sharp. The sound squeezed through vents and under doors and found the men inside like a hand finding a hand.

Marcus's voice came through a cracked window high on the cinderblock, not the words, just the tone—organizing. Andre's laugh blended under it, corralling energy into lanes. You could imagine the scene: Serenity at the rail with Darius on her hip, his cheeks still sticky from tears that had dried into something like awe; Jessica with the megaphone she didn't ask permission to borrow; Kamari leading a row of kids in a call-and-response like a drill team; Tiffany and Brittany flanking, eyes up, mouths steady, a pair of women tired of funerals who had decided tired wasn't the same as done.

Inside, men started clapping to the outside rhythm.

OGs on the downbeat, YNs on the shout. A guard barked "Cut that out," and the clapping got neater, like obedience wrapped in joy. Somebody started the hook of a church song that didn't need a collection plate. Voices joined, layered, harmonized by accident and respect.

Grayson walked the hall once more, his frown trying to reverse-engineer this algebra: anger plus time had equaled unity, not violence; cuffs had become a camera; cells had turned into a choir. He didn't know what to do with that, so he did what men like him always do—checked a box and waited for the box to fix the world.

Paperwork crawled. Names were called in clumps. Lieutenants went first in another life, but here a clerk grabbed whatever stack was on top and read. A Committee YN stepped out, then a Seven OG, then a man who used to be both and now just wanted his knees to stop hurting. The line moved. Calvin could've demanded precedence; he didn't. Reggie could've taken his suit and his headlines outside early; he stayed seated, telling old jokes to men who needed to remember they were still funny.

"Damion Carter! Calvin Price! Reginald Wallace!"

The clerk's voice finally reached their cell. The door buzzed. Metal kissed metal. A deputy opened like he was doing them a favor and a duty both. They stepped out together. Down the hall, past the camera with the red dot, up the stairs that tried to make ankles buckle. At the side door, the deputy hesitated like the world outside might bite. Then he pushed the bar and noise hit them—warm, messy, alive.

The crowd spread from the steps to the curb, signs up, phones out. Westview and Pine Gate mixed into Bricks and Riverstone like watercolors, edges gone, colors richer. When the three men stepped into the night, a wave moved through the people—cheers, tears, the roar of a city refusing to be told what it saw. Serenity was there, eyes wet, chin up, Darius clutching the blue bear and pointing like he'd spotted a constellation. Jessica lifted the megaphone and didn't even need it. Kamari whooped like it was a game-winner. Tiffany and Brittany didn't clap first, but when they did, it was harder than anyone. Marcus and Andre slid to the front, wide shoulders making a lane without touching anybody.

Reggie didn't raise his hands. He raised his voice. "Baymoor," he said, and the crowd leaned like a ship obeying the tide. "They tried to make today a mugshot. Y'all turned it into a march."

Cheers punched the air. A child laughed because her mother did. "We'll talk tomorrow," Reggie said, "at my church. We'll plan. We'll build. Tonight, take your families home and tell them what you did—you stood." He stepped aside. Calvin nodded once—cool, contained, but something in his eyes admitted gratitude to a city he mostly counted. Damion didn't smile big; he gave that same small smirk that had carried him through one set of bars already. He bent, so Darius didn't have to stand on tiptoe to throw both arms around his neck. "I told you I was okay," Damion said into his hair. "You was in jail," Darius accused, muffled. "And now I'm home," he answered, and let the word be true for the space of a breath.

Behind them, Grayson watched from the vestibule, the door

half-closed like he could convince the night to hush. The chant started again, softer now, joyful instead of angry. "Free them all!" turned into "We want peace!" turned into a hum without words that felt like a city remembering its own song.Inside and out had found the same rhythm. The system had to sit with that.

CHAPTER ELEVEN

Baymoor had a way of humming after chaos. Days after the arrests, the city hadn't gone quiet—it had gone *restless*. Reggie Wallace wore that restlessness like a crown. On flyers taped to light poles, on Facebook lives shared in barbershops and corner stores, his name slid into the mouths of people who'd never cared about politics before. *The People's Mayor*, one headline called him. Another said: *Wallace Stands With Baymoor—And Baymoor Stands With Him.* Mothers quoted him in grocery lines. Kids shouted his name on basketball courts. For the first time in a long time, the city felt like it could believe in a suit.

Chief Grayson, meanwhile, had become the villain of every conversation. The phone videos of his march crackdown looped endlessly. He'd meant to break spirits; instead, he'd put himself on trial in the court of public opinion. The hashtags called him a racist. The newspapers called him a disgrace. The city council called him in for closed-door meetings that didn't end with handshakes. He prowled his office like a caged animal, promising himself he'd take his pound of flesh back. And Catherine Price? She felt the ground shift under her designer heels.

Reggie's popularity cut at her campaign. Worse, she'd just learned the Nolans had sold their shares of the casino expansion to the Caldwells—locking her out of a project she thought was already hers. Betrayed and sidelined, she seethed in her office, plotting her next move, chewing on rage like it was bread she couldn't swallow.

It was late, the kind of late where the block got quieter but never truly silent. In the Bricks' park, the basketball rims still rattled from pickup games that had just ended. An old head sat on a bench rolling dice in his palm, not to play, just to hear the sound. Music floated low from a car stereo, bass thumping like a tired heartbeat.

Damion, Marcus, and Andre sat near the court, cooling off from a conversation that kept circling the same theme—what came next. A few younger Sevens lounged nearby, half-watching, half-dozing, always close enough to jump if something snapped. "City love Reggie right now," Marcus said, leaning back, staring at the cracked stars. "He like Baymoor's Obama. Talkin' all smooth, makin' people believe again." Andre smirked. "Better him than Catherine. She look like she chewin' glass every time she on TV." Damion stayed quiet, watching smoke from his cigarette drift toward the playground. He flicked ash, then finally spoke. "It's bigger than them. If the block can stay cool past midnight, maybe... just maybe, Baymoor can breathe. A day without blood buys time." Andre nodded slow. "Yeah, but pride don't sleep. And Tyreek? He ain't been seen since the march. That's what got me watchin' shadows." Marcus laughed once, short. "Boy still salty about you knocking him out in front of everybody." Damion didn't laugh. "Salty men make messy choices."

The words sat there, heavy.

Just before midnight, a car rolled slow down the street, headlights dim. The stereo cut. The air shifted. Every younger Seven on the benches straightened like dogs scenting smoke. The windows slid down. "Down!" Andre barked, diving as the first muzzle flash lit the night. Gunfire spat across the park. Sloppy. Too many bullets, not enough aim. But even sloppy metal finds flesh. Marcus grunted, grabbing his arm as blood spread through his shirt. Damion staggered, hot fire across his side. Kids screamed, mothers on stoops shouted, *"It's the truce!"* Feet pounded against asphalt as the car peeled off into the night.

The park erupted into chaos—voices crying, people cursing, phones already dialing. Someone shouted, "That was them boys from Riverstone" and nobody argued.

Hours later, bandaged and stitched, Marcus and Damion

walked out of the ER together. The wounds were real, but not fatal—meant to scare, not to bury. OGs and YNs waited outside the hospital, faces tight, muttering, asking what happened to the truce. Damion raised a hand, silencing the noise. "No retaliation. Not yet. Calvin gets one last chance. Either he checks Tyreek…" His eyes hardened. "…or we will."
Marcus leaned in, jaw tight. "Last warning. No more passes."

Back at Marcus's shop, Damion pulled his phone. He didn't sit, didn't breathe different. He just dialed. Calvin picked up after two rings. His voice came cold. "I know why you're calling."
Damion's tone was steel. "Your boy just tried to put me in the dirt. Last warning, Calvin. You handle Tyreek, or the Sevens will." Marcus took the phone, heat in his voice. "We let a lot slide. But you know damn well—your nephew almost killed us. If you don't fix this, we will." Silence. Heavy. Then Calvin spoke, voice shaking with fury he wasn't pointing at them. "I'll handle it. Myself."

Later that night, in Calvin's office, Tyreek leaned against a desk, smirking like the night was just another stage he'd owned. "Told you they ain't untouchable. Boys out here scared now." Calvin slammed a fist on the desk so hard a glass cracked. "Scared? You sloppy bastard, you hit *nothing but headlines*. You almost lit a war we can't win." He stepped closer, pointing in Tyreek's face. "You're reckless. Stupid. A liability. And I'm done covering for you. I'm washing my hands of you." Tyreek's smile cracked, then twisted into pride-driven fury. His voice rose, sharp and venomous. "So that's it? You chose money over blood? On my momma, this shit ain't over."

He stormed out, door slamming like a gunshot. Calvin sat back in his chair, breathing fury into silence. He'd cut his nephew loose. But Baymoor wasn't about to let go that easy.

CHAPTER TWELVE

Morning in Baymoor had a particular kind of hunger. It woke with the city and went straight to the gas station on Ash & Third—the one with the line that wrapped past the pump island because the griddle never slept. The breakfast window hissed and sang: bacon crackling, biscuits splitting under steam, egg smell riding the air like a warm hand on the back. Men in safety vests clutched coffees big as thermoses. Nurses in scrubs fished for loose change. A cook in a paper hat shouted orders into the grease like the pan could hear English.

Across the street, a row of kids at the bus stop slouched under backpacks too wide for their shoulders, trading chips and rumors, watching the world like it was a show with too many bad episodes and a few great ones if you caught them live. The sky wasn't all the way blue yet; it wore last night's smoke at the edges. Tyreek pulled up solo, late-model coupe shining, yesterday's arrogance already trying to stretch into today. He slid into the same spot near pump four he always took when he came for a sausage biscuit and attention. He checked his phone, checked his face in the rearview, adjusted a chain that remembered better days.

He didn't look up when Damion turned off the corner, creeping the curb like a thought that had run its course. He'd watched long enough to know routine when it came with syrup. He cut the angle, rolled in, and parked crosswise—a calm, precise move that boxed Tyreek's car in without touching it. In the reflection of Tyreek's window, the street flipped upside down, and then the door opened.

Damion stepped out quiet, not hurried, not angry. His jacket hung open; the Draco rested loose in his hand, low, not for show, not for a lesson—just a set of facts arriving on time. The cook at the window paused mid-spatula. A man in a vest stared, then looked away sharply like he'd remembered a phone call. The kids at the bus stop stopped moving but didn't stop looking. Tyreek's head snapped up. He didn't reach for anything because there was nothing to reach for. No gun on him. No boys. No uncle. Just the morning and the man he'd spent a week pretending not to fear.

"Morning," Damion said, voice even, like the sun had clocked in. Tyreek's mouth moved and didn't find words. A beat. A car hissed past on Third, indifferent. Damion walked until steel and skin were two steps apart, then stopped. He didn't point the weapon. He didn't need to. He let it hang there like truth. "I know you got me hit," he said softly, like he was trying not to wake a baby. "Me and Marcus. Sloppy. You got your little lick back. Congratulations."

Tyreek swallowed. His chest lifted quick, dropped quick, like he'd tried to run without moving. Damion's eyes didn't blink. "You on borrowed time for exactly two reasons—Serenity. And Darius. Remember their names when you go tell lies about what happened here." He tilted his chin toward the bus stop without looking. "You see those kids? They somebody's little God. They at the stage of life where they learn what power look like. You teaching them one thing. I'm teaching them another."

Tyreek glanced over. Four small faces stared back, wide-eyed, frozen. One girl clutched the strap of her backpack like a seatbelt. Damion took a half-step closer. His voice stayed low. "Just like I knocked you out at the fair, I can knock you off right here. You know that. I know that. God know that." He let the words breathe. "But I ain't. Not today. You hit me and Marcus—cool. That's your one. Let that be the end of it before y'all motherfuckers start dying for real. Hear me?" Tyreek nodded, tiny, ashamed of his own neck. "Now," Damion said, "I'ma turn my back, get in my shit, and leave. I'm giving you a chance to do the same. You go to your shit, go with your move if you feel brave—just know you better not miss no more."

The kids at the bus stop held their breath like it could pay rent. At the breakfast window, the spatula finally hit the pan again in a careful rhythm. Somewhere behind them, a church bell took its time finding seven. Damion did what he said: turned his back on a man he could've ended, walked to his car like the earth belonged to people who moved without flinching, and slid in. He backed up slow, giving the exit lane back to the morning. Through the windshield he watched, unreadable.

Tyreek reached for the glovebox although there was nothing in there that could fix humiliation. He didn't get out the car because pride had just discovered gravity. He gripped the wheel, jaw grinding, eyes wet with something he'd never call tears. Then he threw it in gear and peeled out, too hard, too loud, a man trying to outrun a mirror. Across the street, the kids started talking again, voices high and excited, danger rebranded as legend. "He made him punk out," one boy whispered, half awe, half relief. "He ain't even shoot," the girl said, like mercy was a plot twist she didn't expect but might be able to live with.

Damion pulled off cool, left turn signal ticking like a metronome. The phone buzzed on the passenger seat before he cleared the light. Serenity, lit the screen. He answered. "What the fuck going on?" she said without hello. Breath tight. Hurt riding shotgun with fear. "Tyreek just called me, panicking—saying you pulled up on him at the gas station trying to kill him. He said he barely got away." Damion's mouth curved. A low, amused exhale slipped out—less laugh, more the sound of a man who refused to argue with narratives over a wire. "What you want to eat tonight?" he asked. Silence. Then the softest huff, like a smile she didn't authorize. Serenity knew him. Phone was not for confessions. The laugh had answered anyway. Something happened. Something was over. "Pasta," she said finally, voice settling back into its body. "Garlic bread. And a salad so you can pretend you healthy." "Say less," he said. "I'll see you later." "Be careful," she added, quick, quiet, before the call clicked.

As Damion hung up. The light turned green. He rolled through, city yawning open in front of him, the Draco already swallowed back into the dark of the car like a decision postponed. At the bus stop, a kid raised two fingers in a salute he didn't know the rules for yet. Damion tapped the horn once—I see you—and kept going. In the rearview, the gas station shrank to a box of color and steam. Morning finished rinsing the night off the sky. Somewhere on another street, Tyreek drove too fast, heat rising in his face, alone for the first time since he learned how to be loud. He rehearsed a story he could live with and found it didn't fit.

Mercy had a way of echoing louder than shots. The kids would take it to school. The men at the breakfast window would take it to lunch. By dinner, Baymoor would have a new version of what power looked like: not a scream, not a headline, just a man who could end a life and chose to leave.

CHAPTER THIRTEEN

The smell of garlic and butter drifted through Serenity's kitchen like a promise. Damion stood over the stove in a fitted white tee, stirring pasta with one hand and sipping a beer with the other. The sound of Darius's laughter carried from the table where he sat with Serenity, a grin on his chocolate face as he snuck bites of bread before dinner. "Boy, wait till it cool," Serenity said, smacking her lips in mock frustration. "Let him rock," Damion said, flashing a smirk. "That's how you know the food hittin'—when he can't wait."

Darius beamed, proud to be Damion's taste-tester.

They ate together at the small table, voices overlapping, soft warmth filling the space. The kind of dinner that felt unremarkable to anyone else, but to them, it was weighty normalcy they hadn't known how to ask for. After plates were cleared, Serenity tapped Darius's shoulder. "Go on, shower, baby. Get ready for bed. We gon' watch a movie in a minute." Darius lingered, throwing a look at Damion, like he wanted permission. Damion chuckled, ruffling his hair. "Go head, lil' man. I'll save you a seat."

When Darius finally padded down the hallway, Damion clicked through movies on the TV, settling on something light. He had just dropped onto the couch when a knock rattled the door. Serenity frowned. "Who is that this late?"

Damion rose, opened the door—and there stood Kamari and Andre, grinning wide. "Well, well, well," Andre said, sniffing the air dramatically. "Look at Chef Carter over here. Saw y'all lil' snaps —figured I'd pull up for a plate before you close the kitchen." Kamari pushed past with a laugh. "Y'all too cute in here, makin'

pasta like it's Valentine's Day. We came to balance it out."
Serenity shook her head but was already laughing. Damion grabbed two extra plates, shaking his head with a smirk. Minutes later, Andre was leaned back with a fork in his hand, groaning with satisfaction. "Damn, bro. You missed your calling. Forget the streets—open a damn restaurant." "Chef Boyar-D," Kamari teased, nearly spitting her drink from laughing at her own joke.

From the hallway, Darius peeked out, eyes wide at the unexpected company. Damion spotted him and crooked a finger. "C'mon, man, don't be shy." Darius shuffled out, but Serenity shot him a look. "Shower. Now." "Aww, let him chill!" Andre called, laughing. "Nope," Serenity said firmly. "Bedtime." Damion leaned down. "I'll come check on you before the movie. Cool?"
Darius gave a reluctant nod, comforted, and disappeared back down the hall. They had just gotten back into a rhythm of jokes when another knock hit the door.

This time it was Marcus and Jessica, arms folded like offended parents.
"Oh, so this what we doin'?" Marcus said. "Secret dinners? Inviting folks and not us?" Jessica shook her head, smiling. "I *know* damn well y'all didn't have my husband out here starving while Kamari and Andre get plates first." The room broke into laughter as Damion waved them in. "Man, y'all somethin' else. Come on." Soon the kitchen table was crowded with plates, cups, laughter bouncing off the walls. It felt like family—loud, messy, real. Marcus wiped his mouth, leaned back, and sighed. "Man, I need a vacation." Jessica's eyes lit up instantly. "Say less. We're going. You said it. It's happening."
"Wait, I ain't mean—"
"Too late," Jessica cut him off, clapping her hands. "I been waiting for you to say that. Y'all hear this? Pack your bags."

The table roared with laughter. Andre co-signed. Kamari added fuel. Serenity covered her face, shaking her head but smiling. Even Damion couldn't hide his smirk. "Vacation, huh?" he said.
Marcus shrugged. "Hell yeah. East Bay. My family got the beach

house, you know. Sun, water, good food. And I'm getting on my boat. It's been too long." Talk turned serious fast—who was bringing what, what time they'd leave, how long they'd stay. A joke had grown roots. By the end of the night, it was settled: they were leaving tomorrow.

As the crowd thinned and laughter lingered in the air, Serenity caught herself staring at Damion. He fit right in —laughing with Marcus, trading jokes with Andre, deflecting Kamari's sass like a veteran, humbling Jessica's quick tongue with a smirk. For the first time, she saw him not just as the man from her past or the boy tied to the streets, but as a man who could sit at her table and belong. And she wasn't sure whether that scared her more... or made her feel at home.

CHAPTER FOURTEEN

The blinds leaked sunlight into Serenity's living room, thin stripes of gold across the carpet. The house still smelled faintly of garlic and butter from the night before. Serenity moved through the kitchen in a soft robe, humming as she flipped bacon, while Damion sat at the table scrolling his phone, coffee steaming in front of him. Darius darted around in socks, a ball of energy that didn't match the calm morning. He tugged at Damion's arm. "We still going to the beach, right? You said we was going." Serenity leaned on the counter, smiling but steady. "Baby, you not going this time. You're going to Grandma and Grandpa's." Darius's face scrunched. "That's not fair! I wanna go with y'all."

Damion put the phone down, pulled him close. "Lil' man, listen. You gon' have fun in Westview, trust me. And when I come back, I'ma bring you something better than any toy in that gas station you love." He tapped his chest. "You my word." Darius narrowed his eyes like he was testing the promise. Then, slowly, he nodded. Before the moment could stretch, a knock hit the door. Serenity wiped her hands and opened it. Her parents stood there—her father with his firm jaw, her mother with warm eyes but sharper ones for Damion. "Morning, baby," her mother said, wrapping Serenity in a hug before reaching for Darius. "Come on, sweetheart, you ready to ride?" "No," Darius muttered, clinging tighter to Serenity. His grandfather bent down, voice low and steady. "It's just a few days. We gon' spoil you rotten. Then you'll come back talkin' about how boring we are."

The women laughed lightly. Damion crouched down. "Go on, man. Hold it down for me. I'ma need a report when I get back." That cracked the boy's stubborn mask. He threw his arms around Damion's neck, then Serenity's waist, before finally letting himself be led out. He kept waving until the car turned the corner. The house felt quieter, emptier, but not for long. A horn blared outside. "Y'all better be ready!" Marcus's voice carried through the open window. Serenity rolled her eyes and opened the door just as Marcus climbed out of his truck, cooler strapped down in the back. He wore shades like he was already at sea. Jessica trailed behind with a notepad and pen like a general inspecting her troops.

"Alright," Jessica announced, "we need blankets, snacks, chargers, sunblock, and somebody better not forget the towels." Marcus groaned. "Jess, I just said 'vacation.' Didn't mean run a whole grocery list." "Should've kept your mouth shut then," Kamari's voice chimed as she strutted up the walkway in a floppy beach hat and oversized shades. Andre followed, carrying two bags, grumbling under his breath. Damion smirked. "She packed like we leaving the country." Kamari tilted her head. "Excuse me, I pack for *vibes*. Don't hate 'cause you probably only got jeans and Timbs in your bag."

The whole porch erupted in laughter. Jessica clapped her hands. "Here's how we doing this. Girls in the car with me. Boys in the truck with Marcus. Last one there cooks *and* cleans tonight." "Oh, bet," Marcus said, grinning as he slapped the hood of his truck. "Y'all gon' be scrubbing dishes." "Boy, please," Kamari shot back. "Don't stall your old-ass truck on the highway." More trash talk flew as bags were hauled out. Serenity loaded her suitcase into Jessica's car, shooting Damion a side glance—half playful, half warning. He caught it, smirk tugging at his lips, then tossed his duffel into Marcus's truck bed.

By the time engines started, the block was alive with laughter, two cars humming like a convoy about to set out on an adventure. Marcus revved the engine, Andre leaned out the window clowning, Kamari rolled her eyes behind tinted shades, and Jessica shouted directions even though she was the one driving with GPS.

Serenity slid into the backseat of Jessica's car, exhaling as she looked out the window. For a moment, she let herself enjoy the sound of everyone's voices overlapping—loud, teasing, alive. She glanced back toward Damion in the truck, watching him laugh at something Marcus said. And for the briefest second, it felt like they were all on the same page, heading in the same direction, toward something lighter.

CHAPTER FIFTEEN

The beach house sat quiet at the edge of East Bay, clapboard siding sun-bleached and the porch wrapped wide like it had been waiting on family for years. It wasn't flashy. No marble, no chrome. Just wood that creaked right, couches that swallowed you whole, and the smell of sea salt sneaking through the windows. The ladies got there first, Jessica leading the charge with Kamari right behind her. They popped the trunk, dragging bags up the steps like they owned the

Place. "Winners get first pick of the rooms," Jessica announced, her voice bouncing through the hall as she swung the door open. Kamari tossed her shades higher on her head. "And don't say nothing when we take the good ones, 'cause y'all lost fair and square."

By the time Marcus's truck rolled up, tires crunching the gravel, laughter was already spilling out the open windows. Andre hopped down first, shaking his head. "They in here actin' like they built the damn house," he muttered.

Marcus smirked, pulling the cooler out the bed of the truck. "Let 'em talk. I got the grill. That's the throne anyway." Damion came last, duffel slung over his shoulder, half a grin tugging at his mouth as Serenity leaned out the doorway, eyes soft, shoulders loose like she'd already slipped into vacation mode.

Inside, the rooms claimed themselves. Jessica and Marcus took the master without argument; Marcus shrugged, Jessica winked like she'd never even needed permission. Andre and Kamari slid into the side room, bickering about who was unpacking what. Serenity led Damion down the hall and into a smaller room, and for the first time there was no pause, no hesitation she set her bag down like it was second nature, like he was supposed to be there.

When they all circled back to the kitchen, Jessica cleared her throat. "Y'all remember the bet. Losers cook." Marcus puffed his chest. "Main course on me. Barbecue. I'ma bless y'all." Andre threw his hands up. "Sides then. Mashed potatoes, salad—simple and efficient." All eyes cut to Damion. He leaned against the counter, smirk playing at his lips. "Prison honeybun cake." The room exploded. Kamari doubled over. "Predictable as hell!" Jessica nearly spit her drink. "Not commissary cuisine on vacation!" Even Marcus chuckled, shaking his head. "Bruh, you can't leave the block behind, can you?" Damion shrugged, unfazed. "Y'all laugh now, but watch how fast you scrape the pan clean." Serenity, leaning against the wall, cut through the noise, her tone soft but clear. "That cake kept you sane in there. I wanna taste it."

The laughter quieted just a little, the weight of her words hanging between them. Damion's smirk shifted into something smaller, more private. He tapped the counter once and let it drop. Out back, Marcus went to work, meat spread across the table, seasoning shaking down like rain. Andre hovered, half-helping, half-running his mouth. "You know you putting too much salt on that, right?" "Boy, please," Marcus said, not looking up. "I been doing this since before you knew how to tie shoes." Inside, the living room turned into a spades table. Jessica dragged Damion to her side. "You my partner. I need somebody with sense, 'cause Serenity and Kamari swear they the queens." "Oh, we don't swear," Kamari shot back, shuffling with attitude. "We got proof. Remember the last time we ran y'all off the table? Even Asia had to laugh."

Serenity leaned forward, eyes glinting. "Y'all about to lose again tonight."

Cards slapped. Trash talk filled the air. Jessica tried to keep her cool, Kamari hollered after every book, Serenity leaned back smug, and Damion sat calm, letting his silence do the talking as he stacked quiet wins. By the time the sun leaned low, smoke rose from the grill, curling into the evening air. Marcus flipped ribs with a practiced hand. Andre set up a chessboard on the patio table, calling his next win before the first piece touched wood. Inside, spades cards hit the table with the rhythm of dominoes, laughter breaking through the walls. The house was alive: wood creaking under the weight of voices, barbecue smoke sweet on the breeze, the illusion of peace painted thick across the night. For the moment, it felt like family. Like vacation. Like nothing outside those walls could touch them.

CHAPTER SIXTEEN

The morning was wide open, sunlight spilling heavy across East Bay. The crew rolled out of the beach house with the kind of energy only a vacation morning could give—bags of snacks clutched under arms, coolers bumping against knees, Bluetooth speaker tucked under Jessica's arm, Kamari snapping pictures before they even made it down the porch. Marcus locked the front door, chest puffed like he was leading a parade. Jessica slid her shades over her eyes, keys jingling in her hand. "Oh, by the way," she said lightly, as if it was nothing, "I invited Asia to come ride with us. She stays right here in East Bay. Been forever since I seen her."

The group caught it, no problem. Marcus nodded like it made sense. Andre shrugged as he shifted the cooler to his other arm. Kamari smirked but didn't say a word. Serenity tucked the thought away, but her face stayed cool, unreadable. Damion didn't react at all, carrying her bag down to Marcus's truck like he hadn't even heard it. No tension. No questions. They just kept moving.

The docks were alive by the time they pulled up. Gulls wheeled overhead, their cries mixing with the smell of salt and fried food drifting from a shack down the way. Boats bumped against the pier, ropes creaking, water slapping against wood. Marcus strutted down the dock with his chin high, pointing at the white boat rocking gently against the pier. Its paint was faded but clean, the Carter name scrawled across the side. "Captain Carter, baby!" he yelled, spreading his arms. "Y'all don't even know, this about to be the smoothest ride of your life." "Boy, please," Jessica muttered, rolling her eyes. "Just don't crash into the first rock you see."

Andre bent to wrestle a rope loose, fumbling like he had a clue. The line whipped free and nearly dragged him forward into the water. Kamari screamed, phone halfway up, already recording. "Clumsy ass!" she shouted between laughs. "Shut up," Andre grinned, steadying himself. Serenity leaned against the railing, drink in hand, eyes closed as the breeze touched her skin. Damion stood beside her, quiet, watching the horizon like it belonged to him. That's when Asia showed up.

She came casual—cut-off shorts, sneakers, hair pulled into her natural ponytail. Her beauty wasn't loud; it just eased into a space and made it softer. But she wasn't alone. Walking beside her was her younger brother, Malik Johnson. His Baymoor High jersey clung to his frame, tall now, shoulders filling out. Marcus lit up the second he saw him. "Lil' bro!" he hollered, breaking into a grin and pulling Malik into a hug. "Man, look at you! Taller than me now. You still hoopin'? Still runnin' track?" "Both," Malik answered, pride in his grin. "That's what I'm talkin' about," Marcus said, clapping his shoulder. "Y'all don't even know, I been mentoring this boy since he was knee-high. Look at him now. East Bay's finest!"

The crew clapped him up, good vibes spilling easy. Asia hugged Jessica first, the kind that came with years of shared summers. She hugged Kamari next, then Serenity. Serenity's smile was polite and warm, no tension yet.

Once the ropes were off, Marcus took the wheel like he'd been born for it. Jessica clowned him every time the boat rocked too hard, while Andre pretended to know what he was doing with knots and Kamari filmed the whole thing for her story.

The boat pulled away from the dock, engine humming, waves chopping under the hull. Music spilled from the Bluetooth speaker —old R&B that made the ride feel like it could stretch forever.

Andre cracked open the foil on the catered wings he'd brought, grinning like a proud provider. "See? Y'all gon' thank me for this. Vacation food, no dishes." The smell filled the air, mouths watered, and soon everybody was eating, grease slicking fingers, laughter spilling over the sound of the waves.

That's when Asia leaned toward Damion, wing in hand, her eyes catching his. "You remember that game?" she asked with a laugh. "Senior year. You ran that touchdown, got clipped at the last second, and flew straight into the cheerleaders. Broke my leg." Damion froze mid-bite, then cracked up, head tilting back as he laughed deep from his chest. "Damn, I did do that. Thought I killed you." "You almost did," Asia teased, her grin wide. "I was laid up in that hospital bed mad as hell. Whole season ruined."

The group chuckled, shaking their heads, already moving on. But Damion leaned forward, wiping his fingers on a napkin. "I remember pulling up to the hospital the next day with flowers and wings. Didn't even know what to say." Asia's eyes glowed with the memory. "Yeah, you was so awkward. Sweet, though."

They laughed together, light, innocent. But the rhythm between them had its own pull, its own quiet current. Serenity caught it. She didn't frown. She didn't interrupt. She laughed when Marcus nearly tipped the boat trying to spin it sharp. She teased Kamari about her camera obsession. She clinked cups with Jessica and cheered when Malik almost slipped trying to stand too fast.

But she saw the way Asia's smile lingered too long when Damion turned his head. She saw the way her eyes stayed on him, soft and steady.

Damion didn't notice. He was too busy leaning back, soaking in the freedom, letting the salt wind clear him out. Serenity didn't ruin the vibe. She tucked the note in her chest and kept on laughing with the rest. By the time the sun dipped low, gold streaked across the water, Marcus had one arm hooked around Malik's shoulders, proud like a father. "Man, you gon' do big things," Marcus said, voice strong. "Keep grinding, don't stop. You hear me?" "I hear you," Malik said, nodding serious. Marcus turned to Asia, grinning. "Come back to the house tonight. Games, drinks, the whole nine. You already part of the crew today, might as well keep it rolling." Asia laughed, nodding. "I'm there."

The boat hummed back toward the dock, water slapping soft against the sides. Serenity leaned back in her seat, drink in hand, smile still on her lips—but her eyes slipped once more toward Asia, watching the way she looked at Damion. She laughed again, louder this time, letting it blend with the music and the voices, hiding the thought for later.

CHAPTER SEVENTEEN —

Night came soft over East Bay, the beach house glowing warm like a lantern. Low music floated through the living room—old R&B with a lazy bass line—while the smell of leftover barbecue still clung to the air. Somebody had reheated ribs, Andre had dragged out the pans of mashed potatoes and salad, and Damion's honeybun cake sat on the counter with a corner already missing, the fork prints criminal.

"Y'all ready?" Jessica sang, sliding a stack of glossy cards across the table. "Rules for Drunk Uno, 'cause some of y'all gon' swear you ain't hear me: Draw Two—sip. Skip—bite of food. Reverse—you pick somebody else to sip. Draw Four—shot. And if you don't say UNO before you hit one card—two shots, and we clapping at you." Kamari clapped already. "Amen."
Andre squinted like the cards had fine print. "What if I got color-blind?" "Drink water, Mr. Science," Jessica said, already shuffling.

They clustered around the table: Marcus with a plastic cup he swore was his "captain's portion," Andre suspicious of every rule, Kamari bouncing in her seat, Jessica dealing like a Vegas croupier. Serenity sat close to Damion, legs crossed, smile relaxed. Asia settled beside Jessica, casual and at ease, swapping small jokes with her and tossing a comment across to Marcus that made him point and laugh: "Exactly! She know me." It started slow, then turned loud. Reverse, Skip, Draw Two—cards slapped like dominoes. The first Draw Four landed on Andre. "Take your medicine," Kamari sang. Andre cut his eyes around the table, already reaching for the bottle. "Y'all set me up."

Damion stayed measured—quiet laugh, slow sips, a little trash talk. He ate a rib when the table made him. He wiped his fingers, then cut a square of honeybun cake and passed the plate. Asia tried hers and whistled. "Okay, Chef Commissary," she teased, eyes bright. "This better than what the streets promised." Laughter rolled. Marcus pointed his cup. "Predictable, but he wasn't lying." Serenity smiled, soft and private, watching Damion —the way his shoulders sat lower tonight, the way his laugh came from somewhere he didn't lock anymore. She let it warm her, then tucked it away like a match she didn't want to waste.

Malik Johnson had stretched out in an armchair with a plate on his chest and was losing a fight with sleep. His jersey rose and fell slow, the day finally catching him. Marcus glanced over every so often, a little paternal pride snagged behind his grin. Uno got meaner—the way all friendly games do with liquor. Jessica got hit with a Skip, grimaced, then took a defiant bite of cake and pointed at Damion. "Don't let them bully you. Stack on they heads." Asia slid him a napkin without looking, still talking to Jessica. "And if they try it again, throw a Reverse. Make Marcus drink his own rules." Marcus threw his hands up, laughing. "Why she always know exactly what to say?"

Serenity clocked the moment: Asia finishing Marcus's sentence, tossing Damion the napkin before he reached, light as breathing. It wasn't a move. It was muscle memory for hospitality. Still—it landed. Serenity filed it under *Noted* and kept playing. Kamari slammed a Draw Four on Marcus like a judge with a gavel. "Shots, captain!" Marcus took it straight, wheezed like a busted accordion, then tried to reverse it into a hug nobody agreed to. The table exploded, everybody leaning on something to laugh easier. Damion tipped his cup against Serenity's knee; she tapped it back with her knuckles, that quiet *we here* exchange that made the room feel clean. "Uno," Asia said, soft. "WHERE?" Andre shouted, suspicious. "She lying." Jessica snatched Asia's last two cards. "Nope, she got it. And you—two shots. You ain't say Uno last round when you had one card; we been letting you slide."

Andre put on a frown like a child. "That's hateful." "Drink

up," Kamari sang, already recording him regretting life. They took shots for the Draw Fours, bites for the Skips, rib bones piling like architecture. The house felt full—of noise, of people who could be family in another universe, of peace wearing sweatpants and socks.

Serenity let herself enjoy it. She laughed for real. She let her shoulder press against Damion's, shared a look with Jessica when Kamari shimmied her shoulders after a win, nodded at Asia when she made Marcus snort-laugh over some childhood story involving a broken bicycle and a crown of thorns bush. Asia blended without pushing, kept to Jessica and Marcus mostly, smiled when Damion cracked dry jokes from the corner of his mouth, and Serenity felt the smallest tug—not jealous yet, not threatened, just aware. Like seeing a cloud on a far horizon and telling yourself it's probably nothing.

The deck reshuffled. Jessica dealt. Cards flicked around the circle. The Bluetooth speaker skipped to another slow jam and the house exhaled. Somewhere down the hall, Malik finally surrendered; his plate slid off his chest and clinked harmlessly on carpet. Marcus stood, draped a throw over him without breaking the game's rhythm, then sat again grinning—caught and teased by Kamari, to the delight of the table.

Serenity's phone buzzed on the table. Unknown number. She glanced at it and almost ignored it, then something in her belly pulled her thumb to accept. "Hello?"

The room kept moving, Andre accusing a ghost of stacking the deck, Jessica shushing him, Kamari narrating for her stories, Asia laughing with her hand over her mouth, Damion calculating his play. The voice on the phone was ragged. "Serenity?" a woman's breath. Tyreek's mother. "Baby—baby, you there?" Serenity straightened. "Yes, ma'am, I'm here." "They—" The sound caught, then broke. "They shot him. My baby—Tyreek—he—" The word dissolved into a sob that had years in it.

The table's sound thinned and stalled like music under water. Damion's head turned. Jessica's cards stopped moving. Kamari lowered her phone without noticing. "Where are you?"

Serenity asked, voice already changing shape. "Where is he?"
"Hospital," the woman sobbed. "Crown General. They working
—but it's—Lord, I don't—" The rest was ocean. Serenity's body
moved before her thoughts did. She stood so fast her chair
scraped. The room's faces opened toward her like flowers shocked
by weather. She set the phone down slow, like it would explode.
Her chest rose, fell. She found Damion first, then Marcus, and
everything snarled.

"This what y'all wanted?" The sentence tore out of her
throat. No warm left in it. "This what you planned? Get him shot,
then run to the beach like it don't smell like blood back home?"
"Serenity—" Damion started, voice low, trying to find her eyes.
"Don't 'Serenity' me," she snapped, heat breaking through her. "He
called me this morning saying you pulled up on him. Now his
mama calling me crying. Y'all think I'm stupid?" Marcus stood,
palms out. "We ain't touch that boy. I swear to God." "Swear to
who?" she shot back. "You think I don't know how this go? You get
hit, then he get hit, then everybody pretend it was nothing but *air*
moving the bullets. You brought us out here to cover it."

Andre stepped up fast, shoulders wide. "Ain't nobody
ordered nothing. We been with you all day. Boat, house, game,
here. You know that."
Serenity's laugh came out wrong, crooked with hurt. "Yeah—and
who been with your phones? Who you text when we ain't looking?
You think I didn't see you laugh when Tyreek called panicking?"
Damion's jaw tensed. He breathed once. Twice. "I told that man to
leave it alone. I left him standing. That's the truth." He held the
table's silence like a wall. "I ain't make no call."

Asia's eyes flicked between faces, then down. Jessica reached
for Serenity's wrist and missed it by an inch. Kamari's mouth
opened and closed, the joke in her dying before it formed. Marcus
took a step he didn't know where to put. Serenity's phone buzzed
again on the table, mean and insistent. She didn't pick it up. Her
eyes were wet but slick with anger more than tears. "I'm going
back," she said, breath cutting. "Now. Y'all can sit here and play
cards." "Serenity—" Jessica tried, softer. She shook her off. Her gaze

slid to Damion—the man who had fit in her kitchen, made her boy laugh, kissed the corners of her peace—and turned sharp as glass. "If he dies..." She couldn't finish the thought. The word itself was a cliff.

The room didn't move. The music hiccupped and forgot itself. Outside, waves kept kissing sand like this was still a normal night. Damion didn't reach for her. He didn't chase. He just stood very still and let the weight stack. Marcus swallowed hard, eyes on the door like he could hold it shut with a look. Asia put her head down and pressed her lips together until they turned white. Malik snored once, oblivious, the only living thing in the room allowed innocence.

Serenity grabbed her keys off the counter with a sound that felt like ending, and the door let her out.

Silence folded over what was left. The Uno cards lay scattered in the hollow where their hands had been. A square of honeybun cake waited on a paper plate, untouched, frosting catching the last light. Somebody's shot glass tilted and didn't spill, holding the line like pride.

The house still smelled like smoke and sugar. But the sweetness had gone thin.

CHAPTER EIGHTEEN

The night broke in half the moment Serenity grabbed her keys. Her chair scraped, her body moved like fire, and before anyone could say a word the door slammed behind her, hard enough to shake the frame. "Serenity!" Kamari's voice cut the air. She was already on her feet, purse in hand. Andre glanced once at Damion, then Marcus, then bolted after her without hesitation. The tires outside shrieked as their car followed hers into the dark.

Inside, the silence felt heavier than any gunshot. The table still held ribs, cake, cards, shot glasses—but none of it looked like joy anymore. Jessica turned on Marcus, her eyes sharper than any blade. "Tell me straight," she said, each word clear. "Did y'all have something to do with this?" Marcus's jaw flexed, his chest rising like he was bracing for a punch. He shook his head once, slow. "On my brother's grave—no. Jess, I swear to God." Her gaze held him, long and searching. Finally, she exhaled, shoulders loosening, though her voice stayed edged. "I believe you."

Damion was already moving, phone out, thumb hitting Calvin's number. The ring barely buzzed once before it clicked alive. "It wasn't us," Damion said, voice steady but fierce. "Whatever you heard about Tyreek—" Calvin cut him off, his tone low, flat, too calm. "We know it wasn't y'all." Click. The line went dead. Damion froze, staring at the phone like it might explain itself. Marcus's brows pulled tight. Jessica crossed her arms, shaking her head. "That was sinister as fuck," she muttered.

Serenity drove like the road owed her. The streets blurred past, lights streaking, the phone buzzing again and again in her cupholder. She didn't look. Damion's name didn't matter anymore. By the time she pulled into the lot at Crown General, her chest was a war drum.

Inside the hospital, chaos tore at the air. Nurses rushed, voices sharp, sneakers squeaking against polished tile. Serenity froze at the sight ahead: Tyreek's mother collapsed in the lobby, wailing, her hands clawing at the floor as women tried to hold her up. "No, no, no! My baby, my baby!" The sound split through Serenity's chest.

At the far wall, a group of Committee OGs stood like statues, arms folded, their faces iron. She searched one of their eyes, begging for a different story. He shook his head once.

That was all. Her stomach hollowed. Her hands shook. The world moved fast around her—alarms, footsteps, shouts—but all she could hear was his mother's scream. She didn't get to see him. He was already gone.

Two days passed like fog. Serenity didn't answer her phone. Not Jessica. Not Kamari. Not even her parents, who kept Darius close at their house. Damion's number had already been blocked. On the third morning, she finally left. She drove into Riverstone Heights, the skyline sharper here, the streets cleaner, where Calvin lived above the city like nothing could touch him. She knocked once, and the door cracked open to him leaning against the frame, shirt loose, pupils blown wide. Her voice came sharp. "That was your nephew. Why you ain't out here asking questions? Why you ain't looking for who did it?"

Calvin's expression didn't change. Detached. Distant. "What you want me to say, Serenity? He made his choices. Streets got rules." Her eyes narrowed. "You gon' sit up here high while his mama crying herself blind?" He sighed, disappearing for a moment, then came back with a brown bag. He held it out like it was nothing. "If you or Darius need anything, I got you." She looked at the bag, then at him. The disgust on her face said everything. "Money? That's all you got for me?" She dropped it back on his counter and walked out, fury riding her heels.

The Bricks breathed heavy that night. Kids darted between corners, women sat on stoops, and the men leaned against cars with eyes that followed everything. Damion was outside, Marcus nearby, when Serenity's car cut in slow. She stepped out like a storm, her face set, her stride straight at him. "Serenity—" Damion started, hands half-raised. Her fist caught his jaw clean before his words finished. He stumbled back, shock flashing across his face. She swung again, fists pounding his chest, tears streaking her cheeks. "Did you know?" Her voice cracked with rage. She hit him again. "Did you know?"

"Serenity!" Damion caught her wrists, not to hurt her, just to hold her. His voice was raw, desperate. "I swear on everything— it wasn't me. It wasn't us." She shook her head, crying harder, her voice breaking. "I don't care. We're done. Don't call me, don't look for me and stay the fuck away from Darius." She shoved him back and turned, storming toward her car.

Damion didn't chase. Marcus shifted like he might but stopped when he saw the way Damion's shoulders dropped, the way the whole block was watching. Serenity slammed the door, engine roared, and then she was gone. The Bricks went quiet, only the hum of streetlights above. Damion stood there, jaw tight, the taste of blood in his mouth, her words heavier than prison. Slow dread hung over the block, thick as smoke.

CHAPTER NINETEEN

The church in Riverstone Heights was overflowing. Black suits and dresses pressed shoulder to shoulder, the air thick with perfume, smoke, and grief. Tyreek's casket sat up front, drowned in white flowers, but the walls could barely contain the weight of the people who came. The Committee was out heavy, filling the front rows. The Sevens stood posted near the back, present but distant. Families from every block in Baymoor slid through to pay respects, their whispers buzzing louder than the preacher's microphone.

Serenity entered quietly, flanked by her parents, Darius's small hand tucked tight in hers. Her face was a mask, cold, unreadable, but her eyes burned red from nights of silence. Darius tugged at her arm, his voice too soft for the heaviness around them. "Mama... why everybody crying?" She swallowed, pulling him closer, unable to answer.

Across the room, Damion sat with Marcus, Andre, Jessica, and Kamari. His gaze found Serenity once, a silent plea across the aisle, but she didn't blink, didn't move, didn't give him even that. She turned her head, her profile sharp as glass. Near the pulpit, Calvin sat alone. A sharp suit, dark shades hiding his eyes, hands clasped in his lap. But behind those glasses, tears slid down, ignored by everyone. His presence felt small, standoffish, almost foreign, like even grief couldn't find him.

The preacher's voice rose about peace, about forgiveness, but the air didn't listen. Tyreek's mother collapsed at the casket mid-service, wailing until the walls shook. In the back, Committee YNs whispered heatedly about retaliation, their words sharper than prayers. Marcus leaned close to Damion, his voice low. "Don't give 'em nothin'. They fishing for a reason." Damion nodded once, jaw tight.

When the service spilled into the streets, grief turned into static. Groups clustered on the steps and sidewalks, cigarettes flaring, voices low but sharp. The city's rumor mill spun fast. "Rusty cut Calvin off the same morning Tyreek got hit," one man muttered, smoke curling from his lips. "No shipment. Said he done with the Committee. You ask me, he lined Tyreek up hisself." Another voice cut in from the other side. "Man, I heard Damion pulled up on Tyreek at that gas station. Had him dead to rights, Draco in hand, but he spared him. So why he gon' double back and get him killed now? That don't add up."   The whispers stacked on each other, stories bending into contradictions. Some said Damion guilty. Some said Rusty playing chess. Nobody knew where the truth ended and the lies began. What mattered was the confusion — and confusion in Baymoor always bled. Not far from the casket, a cluster of Committee OGs watched Calvin. They'd noticed the way he sat detached during the service, eyes glassed, words absent. When they tried to approach him, he brushed them off, barely speaking. His silence felt wrong. One OG shook his head. "Somethin' off with that man." Another spat, "He high as a kite at his nephew funeral. That ain't leadership."
Instead of pressing Calvin further, the OGs turned toward the back — toward Damion and Marcus.

They closed the distance slow, shoulders wide, the crowd parting just enough. One of them leaned in, voice low but sharp enough for others to catch. "The only reason we ain't made a call yet is 'cause we ain't got proof. But if we find out y'all had anything to do with Tyreek's death?" His eyes cut straight into Damion. "It's war." Damion didn't flinch. He didn't speak. Marcus stayed stone-faced beside him. They knew words here would be gasoline. The silence tightened, the crowd holding its breath, waiting for the first spark. That's when Reggie stepped in.

"Enough." His voice carried like a gavel, firm but calm. He put himself between the OGs and the Sevens, his eyes hard. "Ain't the time, ain't the place." One of the OGs sneered. "And what, we just let it slide?" Reggie's tone didn't break. "Catherine Price and Chief Grayson moving pieces y'all aren't even paying attention to. They are cooking something' big and trust me — it's meant to divide us while we blind with grief. Don't let 'em play you." His words didn't heal the wound, but they stalled the blade. The OGs muttered, side-eyed, then backed off into the crowd, tension still snapping in the air.

Serenity left soon after, Darius's hand locked in hers, her parents guiding her down the steps. She didn't look Damion's way once. Calvin lingered on the church steps, shades still on, his suit catching the late sun. Tears slid beneath the lenses, but no one went to him. He looked smaller than ever, the kingpin stripped down to a man no one trusted. Damion stood outside, silent, his jaw clenched, the whispers swirling like storm winds. Rusty's name. His own name. Tyreek's name. Nobody knew the truth, but everybody was ready to believe something Baymoor buried Tyreek today. But in the dirt with him lay secrets, and above ground grew doubt that would not die easy.

CHAPTER TWENTY

Marcus and Jessica's house smelled like family—baked chicken, collard greens, macaroni bubbling in the oven. It was Sunday in Baymoor, and even with the streets humming restless after Tyreek's funeral, the tradition of dinner pulled people together. But not everyone. Serenity had already told Jessica she wasn't coming. Not out of spite, not with sharpness—just with that quiet weight grief leaves behind. Jessica hugged her on the phone, told her to take her time. When Marcus asked later, she just shook her head and said, *"She needs space."*

By the time Damion and Andre arrived, Serenity's parents were already settled in the living room. Marcus's mother was folding napkins, his father fixing his tie even though he didn't need to. The game played low on the TV—commentators murmuring over a highlight reel.

"Boy, come here," Marcus's father said, waving Damion over before Marcus could even greet him. Andre caught the cue instantly, ducking away toward the kitchen. "I'ma go see what the food talkin' about," he said, sliding in next to Marcus and his mother.

Damion followed the older man to a quiet corner. The weight in his eyes was the kind that comes from seeing generations rise and fall.

"I been praying for you," the man said, his voice gravelly, slow, every word intentional. "I see you trying. I see you reaching to be better. Don't think it go unnoticed." Damion nodded once, respectful, but the man wasn't finished.

"God showed me a dream," he continued, speaking in the rhythm of a sermon. "Blessings are waiting for you. Big ones. But blessings come with responsibility. You're almost through your test, son...

don't fail now."

His hand rested heavy on Damion's shoulder. "I know you didn't kill Tyreek. I heard about my baby girl cracking your jaw. She's hurt. But give her time. She'll come around."

Damion swallowed, chest tight. He didn't know what to say, so he just nodded again, slow.

That's when the front door opened. Asia stepped inside with a small smile, greeting Marcus's parents first, her tone warm and polite. She carried herself like she belonged, even if she was still new to the circle. The TV caught her attention—football flashing across the screen. Damion glanced at it too, and without trying, they fell into conversation. "You still think the Cowboys gon' make a run this year?" Asia asked, eyebrow lifted. Damion smirked. "Don't start that. You know they gon' choke."

They laughed lightly, both fixing plates from the kitchen before settling into the living room with the others. Nothing heavy, nothing flirtatious. Just Sunday talk. The air shifted when Kamari walked in. She set her purse down, scanning the room, and her eyes locked on Damion sitting beside Asia.

Her expression said it all: *You bold as fuck.* Damion looked back, confused, brows raised like *What?* Kamari shook her head, lips pressed and walked past him. She fixed herself a plate and slid down next to Andre without another word.

She didn't tell Serenity. Not yet. Instead, she sat quiet, watching. Dinner moved easy after that. Plates filled and emptied. The game played in the background, laughter spilling into the room when Marcus's father got animated over a bad call. Serenity's parents excused themselves after halftime, hugging everyone before slipping out into the night.

Once they were gone, the atmosphere loosened. Bottles came out, cups filled. Kamari leaned over Andre. "You got some backwoods?" Andre shook his head. "Nah, not tonight." Before the pause could grow, Asia's voice cut in. "I got some raw cones." Every head turned. Kamari arched her brow, smirking sharp. "*You* smoke? Ms. Nurse? Ms. Bougie?" Asia shrugged, calm as water. "Keep your smoke. I brought mine. Got a card for PTSD. This strain right here?" She pulled a small jar from her bag, grinning. "They call it *Ghost Train Haze*."

The group chuckled, passing the jar around. Soon the smoke was in rotation, laughter warmer, jokes looser. Even Kamari cracked a smile, almost softening toward Asia. Almost.

By the time the fourth quarter rolled in, the room was hazy, the table cluttered with plates and cups. Everyone leaned back, mellow, the weight of the week temporarily off their shoulders.

Then Asia stretched, standing with her bag in hand. "Hey, Damion. You should swing by the bar tomorrow night. Monday Night Football. I'll make sure you got a seat." It was casual, tossed out like nothing. Damion didn't hesitate. "Bet. I'll pull up."

The words weren't even cold before Kamari's face hardened again, her smile gone. She didn't say anything, but the look she shot across the room could've cut glass.

Damion didn't notice. Or maybe he did, but he stayed silent. The laughter carried on, the smoke lingered, but Kamari's eyes stayed on them both.

CHAPTER TWENTY-ONE

The bar was buzzing low, neon lights humming against brick walls, TVs lined up above the counter blaring Monday Night Football. Damion slipped through the door without fanfare, dap'd a couple familiar faces on his way to the bar, then slid onto a stool like he'd done it a thousand times.

Asia was behind the counter, hair tied up, shirt rolled at the sleeves. She lit up when she saw him. "Right on time. First drink on me."

Damion smirked, taking the glass when she poured. "Appreciate you." They fell into easy talk, eyes drifting to the TV where Baymoor High highlights played on a local sports reel. Malik's name flashed, stats scrolling across the screen.

"You ever think about coaching?" Asia asked, leaning against the bar. Damion raised an eyebrow. "Coaching?" "Baymoor High needs one bad," she said. "Malik's got talent, but no real guidance. Whole program suffers. You? You been in it. You'd be a good fit." Damion chuckled, shaking his head. "I ain't no coach." "Not yet," she pressed. "But you know the game. The kids listen to you. You'd make a difference."

Her words sat heavier than she knew. Damion didn't answer right away, staring at the TV like maybe the idea wasn't so wild.

That's when the door opened. Serenity stepped inside. She was dressed casual, hoodie and jeans, hair pulled back, but the heat in her eyes made the whole bar turn. Beside her was Kamari, chin high, eyes already searching. They had walked in together, but

Kamari had done most of the talking on the drive. Serenity knew everything now—Asia at Sunday dinner, the invite to the bar, Damion agreeing without hesitation.

Serenity's jaw tightened the second she saw him at the counter, leaning into conversation with Asia like the world hadn't just fallen apart.

Kamari's lips twisted, and before Serenity could even move, she spotted **Andre** sitting at a table nearby, beer in hand, laughing too loud at the TV.

"Andre!" Kamari snapped. "What the fuck are you doing here?"

Andre blinked, slow and sloppy. "Watching the game," he slurred, confused. "What you mean?"

The words carried, bouncing across the bar, pulling eyes from every corner. Conversations died. The room leaned in.

Serenity moved slow, each step deliberate, the sound of her sneakers against the floor louder than the commentary on the TV. She stopped just short of the bar, her eyes locked on Damion like he was the only person in the room. "So this what you on?" she said, her voice low, sharp, cutting. "Couldn't even wait a week before moving on?"

Damion sat still, his face calm but tight, his glass untouched. He shook his head once. "It ain't like that. You know it ain't." Asia straightened, her tone calm but firm. "We were just talking football. That's it." Serenity turned her gaze on her, cold enough to freeze the words in her throat. Kamari was right there to pour gasoline. "He sure looked comfortable though."

The silence that followed was heavier than noise. People at nearby tables turned back to their drinks, whispering, side-eyes darting between Serenity and Damion. The game on TV might as well have been static.

Damion and Serenity's eyes locked, years of history and pain pressed into one moment.

Serenity's lip trembled before she pressed it tight. She muttered something under her breath—low, sharp, final—then turned on her heel. Kamari followed, her smirk faint but satisfied, tossing one last glare at Damion before disappearing through the door.

Damion stayed seated, jaw clenched, staring into his glass without drinking. His chest burned, but he refused to let it show.

Asia lingered, the crowd's whispers still curling in the air. She looked at Damion differently now, realizing she'd walked into something messy, something raw, something bigger than her. The bar returned to noise, but for Damion, the night was already over.

CHAPTER TWENTY-TWO

Baymoor woke up to blue lights. Sirens screamed down Main Street before sunrise, news vans clogged the courthouse steps, and phones buzzed with the same headline before breakfast:

Committee soldier Jamal "Stacks" Rivers arrested for the murder of Tyreek Johnson.

The official story was neat—too neat. Police called it a "botched robbery," a street deal gone sideways. But Baymoor had ears everywhere, and nobody believed it. In the Bricks, in Riverstone Heights, at the docks—every corner whispered their own version. "Stacks ain't move without somebody telling him." "Man was jealous, Tyreek had all the shine, all the girls." "Nah, Rusty cut Calvin off the morning Tyreek died. That can't be coincidence."

Rumors twisted like smoke, pointing in every direction but never settling. At Serenity's kitchen table, the news hit different. Her father folded the paper in half, slapped it on the table. "Told you that boy Damion ain't do it." The words landed sharp. Serenity sat with her coffee cooling in her hands, staring through the steam.

Every scene replayed in her head: the funeral, her fists on Damion's chest, the way his voice cracked when he swore innocence.

Her stomach knotted. She had swung at the wrong man. Kamari sat across from her, quiet, watching. She didn't smirk, didn't gloat, just sipped slow from her mug. Serenity felt the apology rise in her throat but couldn't push it past her lips.

In the Bricks, Marcus's barbershop was louder than a stadium. Clippers hummed, the TV blared the local news replaying Stacks's mugshot, and voices overlapped like waves crashing. "They really got Stacks for it." "Man, he wasn't stupid enough to shoot Tyreek without orders." "Y'all blind—Stacks hated that boy. Always jealous."

Damion sat quiet in the corner chair, arms folded, jaw set. He didn't say a word, didn't give them a headline. He just let the noise pass over him. Marcus walked over, clapped a heavy hand on his shoulder. "See? Truth don't need no lawyer—it stands on its own." Damion gave him a nod, but his eyes never softened. In Baymoor, even the truth carried weight you couldn't shake off.

Outside City Hall, Reggie Wallace was ready. The cameras loved him; the mic caught every word. "The arrest of Jamal Rivers proves what I've been saying from the start. The Sevens did not retaliate. They've been painted as villains by people in power who profit off division. Catherine Price, Chief Grayson—Baymoor deserves better than your lies."

Supporters cheered behind him, signs lifted high. His mayoral stock climbed with every flash of the camera. Across the street, Catherine watched from the courthouse steps, lips tight, eyes sharp. She didn't clap, didn't blink. Her silence was its own kind of threat.

That night, Serenity sat in her car outside her boutique, the dashboard light dim, her phone glowing in her hand. Her thumb hovered over one name.Damion. She wanted to call. She couldn't. Instead, her fingers typed quick, heart pounding. *I'm sorry.* Two words. No more, no less. She hit send.

In the Bricks, Damion's phone buzzed against the counter. He picked it up, screen lighting his face. The message stared back at him.

His jaw tightened, but he didn't type back. Not tonight. The barbershop buzzed in the distance, the city still whispering, but in his hand, those two words weighed heavier than all of it.

CHAPTER TWENTY-THREE

Baymoor exhaled after Stacks's arrest, but it wasn't peace —just a long breath between storms. The Sevens walked a little lighter in the Bricks now that Damion's name was clearing, but Riverstone Heights was restless. The Committee split itself down the middle: Some whispered Calvin had a hand in Tyreek's death —too calm at the funeral, too detached, too slow and fogged to act like a grieving uncle. Others swore Stacks acted alone, jealousy burning hot, tired of Tyreek's flash and attention. Either way, trust inside the Committee cracked. No united front.

At the barbershop, clippers buzzed steady. The TV replayed the same highlights, but conversation rolled over it. "Serenity cracked him in front of everybody," a young Seven said. "I don't know if I could've took that," another muttered. One of the older ones shook his head. "What was he supposed to do? Everybody knew he ain't do it. Now Stacks locked up—she know she was wrong." The room nodded. Damion stayed silent in the corner chair, arms folded, unreadable.

Later, when the shop emptied out, he pulled out his phone. That same message glowed at the top of the screen: I'm sorry. His thumbs hovered, typed *It's cool*. Deleted. Typed *We good*. Deleted. He locked the screen, face blank, and slid the phone back into his pocket.

On the other side of town, Serenity buried herself in the boutique. Mannequins dressed clean, racks straight, Darius coloring at the little table by the window. Work kept her moving, but nights stayed heavy. She'd lie awake, hearing her own voice cracking against Damion's chest, seeing the look in his eyes when she didn't believe him.

Kamari showed up one evening with takeout. She curled onto the couch, tone softer than usual. "Damion gon' come around," she said. "Andre told me he wasn't on that with Asia, and Asia wasn't either. She was working most the time."Serenity pressed her lips tight.

Kamari sighed. "I'm sorry for how that bar night played out. I thought I was protecting you. Didn't mean to make it worse." Serenity nodded slow, her eyes glassy but grateful. "Thank you." They ate in quiet, TV whispering nothing in the background.

Across Baymoor, in an office with the blinds drawn, Catherine Price sat across from Chief Grayson. Their words were low, clipped. Catherine's nails tapped against the folder on the desk. "Reggie's ahead in the polls," she said.

Grayson's mouth curled sharp. "Then it's time people remember who keeps order."

They didn't say much. They didn't need to. Whatever they were planning smelled like smoke before the fire.

By Saturday, Jessica made her call.

"Sunday dinner at my house," she told Serenity. "I don't know if I'm ready," Serenity said, staring out the boutique window. "Baby, you can't avoid forever." The silence stretched until Serenity snapped. "Did you try to hook them up? Damion and Asia—did you...?"

Jessica didn't flinch. "I didn't do shit. They was talking football. Damion went on his own. Asia ain't invite him like no date." Serenity's breath wavered. "Jess, I—" Jessica cut her off, laughing it away. "Bring my nephew to get his pie Sunday. You know he love my pecan pie."

A reluctant smile tugged Serenity's lips. "He do." "See you Sunday." Click.

That night, Baymoor was quiet, but not settled. In the Bricks, Damion sat on his bed, phone in hand, staring at the black screen. Across the city, Serenity lay in hers, staring at the glow of her own.

Two silences. Same weight.

CHAPTER TWENTY-FOUR

The smell of charcoal and seasoning wrapped Marcus and Jessica's Westview home like a welcome sign. Out back, the grill smoked heavy with ribs and chicken, Marcus working the tongs with a beer in his free hand. From the kitchen, the sound of hot grease popping meant Jessica was frying fish the way everybody in Baymoor swore only she could. Westview gave the night a different energy. Unlike the Bricks or Riverstone Heights, this was neutral ground. Marcus's house had always been a safe spot—far enough from the city's tension for people to breathe without looking over their shoulders.

The living room TV blasted Sunday football while Sevens filled the couches, talking trash with plates in their hands. Serenity and Kamari sat with a few Bricks women near the dining room, kids running through the hall with sticky fingers and laughter trailing behind them. Every so often, Serenity glanced toward the backyard where Damion stood with Andre, dapping up other Sevens, but she kept her space. They exchanged nods, cordial, nothing more.

The gate out back creaked open. Andre walked in with two older men at his side—Committee OGs. They weren't dressed like soldiers, but like fathers: polos tucked into jeans, work boots clean, shoulders broad from years of labor.

Their wives followed, arms looped, carrying warm smiles and store-bought pies. The backyard paused for a beat. Younger Sevens posted up at the patio table leaned back, eyes narrowing. Their silence was heavy, but their respect was intact. This was

Marcus's house, and nobody disrespected Marcus's house.

Marcus set down his tongs and stepped forward, big grin cutting through the smoke. "Man, look at this. My boys from way back. Come on in, we got plates waiting." Hands clasped, shoulders hugged, tension thinned. Later, plates full and cups poured, the talk turned heavier. The two Committee men leaned in, voices low but steady. "Real talk," one said. "We dry. Calvin... he been trippin'. Ain't moving like a leader. And Rusty?" He shook his head. "He never trusted us. Kept us out the loop from the start." The second man glanced between Marcus, Andre, and Damion. "We ain't come here to cause no static. We just asking... can y'all get us a sit-down with Rusty? Just a conversation. Something."

Damion stayed silent, sipping slow, eyes sharp. Andre scratched his jaw, looking toward Marcus. Marcus leaned back, voice calm, respectful. "I'll see what I can do. Let y'all know something." The words were smooth, but in his chest, he knew the truth—Rusty wasn't taking that meeting. Not in this lifetime. The weight broke when the game inside roared at a touchdown. Laughter rolled out, and the smell of fish carried through the sliding door. Soon the backyard was all chatter and chewing, the edge softening under full bellies and strong drinks.

The Committee OGs' wives sat with Jessica, Serenity, and the Bricks women. They swapped recipes, laughed about reality TV, traded gossip about local folks. For a moment, it sounded like any other Baymoor kitchen, no colors, no corners. Serenity leaned back, watching the mix. She noticed Damion laughing with Marcus and Andre, noticed the Sevens dapping the Committee men like brothers. She stayed out the way, giving him space, but inside she felt something she couldn't quite name—maybe relief, maybe unease.

The younger Sevens never stopped watching, eyes sharp, but they didn't say a word. Respect hung thicker than the smoke. By the time the game wound down, the night mellowed. Plates stacked, music dropped lower, kids started yawning. The two Committee OGs stood, wives gathering purses. "Appreciate y'all opening the door for us," one said, his tone humble. "Food was on point. We won't forget it." "Yeah," the other added. "Meant something to sit here, break bread like this. Respect."

Marcus shook their hands firm. Andre clapped them on the back. Damion gave a slow nod, his silence carrying weight. They walked out the gate, humble and grateful, leaving before pride could stir the air. When the gate clicked shut, the backyard settled. The younger Sevens relaxed, women gathered plates, and the sound of the football game bled soft from the living room.

Damion stood a moment longer, beer bottle sweating in his hand, eyes following the taillights as they disappeared down the quiet Westview street. For one night, the line between Sevens and Committee blurred. They'd eaten, laughed, shared space like men instead of enemies.

But Damion knew better than to trust nights like this. Peace never stayed long in Baymoor.

CHAPTER TWENTY-FIVE

The last of the Committee OGs and their wives slipped through the gate, their thanks still echoing as the night settled. The backyard grew quiet, grill smoke thinning into the Westview sky. Inside, Jessica and the other women cleared plates while the TV carried on about the fourth quarter. Damion stayed outside, leaning against the porch rail with a beer in his hand, eyes fixed on the street like he was waiting for something that wasn't coming. His face was calm, but there was a distance in him, a silence that weighed more than any words.

Through the glass door, Serenity watched him. For a long moment, she stood still, her chest tight, the sound of laughter and clinking dishes behind her. No one pushed her. Jessica didn't say a word. This was her choice. She slid the door open, the night air brushing against her. Damion didn't turn. "Can I talk to you?" Serenity's voice was low, careful.

Damion sipped his beer before answering. "You already are." She came closer, folding her arms against the chill. "I was wrong." Her eyes lingered on the ground, then on him. "Everything with Tyreek... I let my anger talk for me. I didn't give you a chance." Damion chuckled dry, no humor in it. "Nah, Ne-Ne. You abandoned me. Again." Her head lifted, eyes narrowing. "What you mean 'again'?" He finally looked at her, eyes sharp. "When I was locked up. You disappeared for months. Letters stopped. Calls unanswered. You went ghost on me. You think I ain't feel that? You think I ain't know?"

Serenity swallowed, guilt pressing heavy in her throat. "I

wasn't strong enough. I was drowning, Damion. Every day felt like waiting for the bottom to drop. I couldn't hold you up and keep myself together at the same time." Damion shook his head slow. "Yeah, but you didn't even try. Left me in there wondering if you'd moved on. Now I'm out, and soon as shit got messy—you did it again."

Tears stung her eyes, but she held them back. "I know. And I hate it. That's why I came out here, to tell you I'm sorry. Not just for Tyreek. For before too." They stood in silence, the night pressing in around them. Inside, a burst of laughter carried through the glass—Jessica and Asia sharing a story.

Serenity's eyes flicked that way, then back to Damion. "What's up with you and her?" she asked, voice edged. "Asia. You said more words to her tonight than you said to me." Damion's jaw tightened. "It ain't like that." Serenity crossed her arms. "Then what is it?" "She asked me about the game," Damion said, his tone even. "That's it. Don't make it more than it is." Serenity studied his face, searching for cracks. "You sure, about that?"

Damion's eyes didn't waver. "I ain't gotta be sure. I know. She ain't you. And I ain't never looked at her like that." Her lip trembled before she pressed it tight. She turned her head, looking out at the street. "I just needed to hear it to your face. I'm sorry, Damion." He nodded once, but the wall between them stayed. "Yeah." Serenity let out a breath she didn't know she was holding. Serenity walked back toward the sliding door, brushing past Asia on her way in without a word.

Damion stayed outside, beer sweating in his hand, eyes on the empty street. The grill was cold now, smoke long gone, but the weight of it all still hung in the night.

CHAPTER
TWENTY-SIX

The clippers buzzed, low and steady, like a soundtrack for the day. Marcus leaned over a chair, lining up a teenager's fade while ESPN highlights played on the mounted TV. The shop smelled like alcohol spray and aftershave, the air thick with voices and laughter. It started with a phone notification. Somebody in the chair pulled out their phone, thumbed the screen, and held it up. "Y'all seen this? Marcus posted last night—look." The screen showed a picture: Marcus, Andre, and Damion, arms locked with a pair of older Committee OGs in polos, smiles stretched wide. The caption: **Unity.**

The room shifted.

One of the older Bricks guys, gray creeping into his beard, let out a whistle. "Boy, Baymoor ain't gon' know how to act. Sevens and Committee at the same table? Eating ribs? That's news." A younger Seven laughed. "Man, they look like they ready to run for office or somethin'." Another YN leaned forward. "Nah, for real, that's big. Word already spreading like wildfire. Folks sayin' the beef dead, truce real now that Tyreek gone."

The shop buzzed with overlapping voices—hopeful, excited, even proud. Then one of the Bricks OGs leaned back in his chair, voice dropping low. "Y'all hear about Calvin, though?" The room quieted just enough.

Two YNs exchanged a look. One spoke up. "We went to check on him last night. Man... he gone. Zooted out his mind. Paranoid like he seein' ghosts. We ask him about Tyreek, about gettin' back, about the OGs eatin' with y'all—he couldn't even talk straight. Just mumblin', lookin' at the walls."

The other YN shook his head. "Ain't the Calvin we grew up respectin'. That was... somethin' else. Had me feelin' weird, bro." A murmur spread through the shop. "That's what happen when you mix money and powder too long," one OG muttered. "Yup. Committee fallin' apart right in front of us."

The conversation swung back lighter for a moment, somebody cracking a joke about Marcus's grill skills in the Unity pic. "Boy, you ain't put no love in that plate—look at Damion face. He look like he wanted to fight the ribs."

Laughter rolled through the shop, easing the weight. Andre grinned, shaking his head. "Y'all gon' stop playin' on my brother. That food was hittin', ask anybody." "Yeah, hittin' the trash can," a YN fired back, and the whole shop roared.

When the noise calmed, one of the Bricks OGs spoke again, his tone heavier. "Jokes aside, y'all peep Catherine and Grayson? Don't think they ain't watchin'. Reggie out here lookin' like the people's champ, and y'all postin' 'Unity' pictures? That's gon' rattle cages. They gon' scheme somethin' dirty. Mark my words." The younger ones fell quiet, letting the weight settle.

Marcus snapped his clippers off, brushing loose hair from his client's shoulders. "That's the thing about Baymoor," he said. "Every time we build somethin' solid, somebody outside lookin' to tear it down." Heads nodded. Damion hadn't said much, just sat in the corner chair, eyes sharp, listening. He let the words soak, like he was carrying them deeper than anybody else.

The doorbell chimed. Heads turned. Asia stepped inside, sunlight catching her in all the right places. Hair laid perfect, outfit clean and tailored, heels clicking against the shop floor. Every conversation stumbled into silence.

One of the YNs whispered, "Damn..." under his breath.

She smiled politely, scanning the room, then her eyes landed on Damion. The quiet stretched, heavy and unexpected. The shop that had just been buzzing with rumors, jokes, and warnings now sat still, caught off guard by beauty and tension

walking through the door.

CHAPTER TWENTY-SEVEN

The barbershop buzz had slowed to background noise—clippers humming, TV low, small talk scattered. Then the door swung open and Asia walked in. She wasn't loud about it, didn't come in making a scene, but the way she carried herself—the heels, the fit, the confidence—turned heads without trying. Even the younger Sevens who'd been cracking jokes earlier sat up straighter.

She offered Marcus a warm smile, then crossed the room like she knew exactly where she was going. Straight to Damion. He raised an eyebrow when she pulled a slim envelope from her bag and pressed it into his hand. "What's this?" Her smile widened, playful but calm. "Call it a thank you. You said take Baymoor over the spread. I put down five and walked out with ten. That's three for you."

Damion chuckled, shaking his head. "I ain't no bookie, Ne-Ne. Keep your money." Asia pushed the envelope back toward him, voice soft but firm. "I don't need it. You earned it. Don't argue with me." Damion exhaled, still smiling, slightly impressed. He slid the envelope into his jacket, more to end the back-and-forth than anything. "Alright, alright. But next time, I'm charging commission upfront."

She laughed quietly, then turned toward Marcus with a polite nod. "Appreciate you, big bro." With that, she smoothed her skirt, and slipped out as gracefully as she had walked in.
The bell over the door chimed shut.

For a long moment, the shop stayed silent. Clippers buzzed.

Nobody said a word.

Marcus finally looked up from his chair, eyes steady on Damion. No smile. No jokes. Just that look. Damion lifted his hands slightly. "It ain't like that. She just came to—" Marcus cut him off, voice low but sharp. "Don't explain it to me. It ain't my business. Just don't let it become my business." The weight in his tone lingered heavy between them.

Damion leaned back in his chair, still smirking faintly, but the warning sat in the air like smoke that wouldn't clear. The shop's hum picked up again, but nothing felt the same.

CHAPTER TWENTY-EIGHT

The shop was still settling after Asia left, the quiet heavier than the smell of alcohol spray and burning clippers. Marcus had gone back to lining up a head, Damion leaning in his corner chair, when a younger Seven pulled out his phone.

"Yo, y'all seen this live? Shorty in Riverstone got the whole block watching."

Heads turned as he tilted the screen toward the room. The sound filled the shop: a woman's steady voice cutting through chaos. Sirens wailing. Lights flashing against rowhouse windows. Boots pounding pavement. "They outside Calvin spot right now," she said, her camera jerking as she stepped backward to catch the scene. "Whole Feds out here, vans and everything. They takin' the Committee down tonight."

The screen shook as neighbors yelled, some laughing, some cursing. Still, the woman held her phone high, narrating like she'd been waiting for this moment. Then the front door burst open on the live. Calvin stumbled out, cuffed, shoulders slumped, head hanging. His clothes wrinkled, face slack, eyes glassy and gone. He looked less like the feared hustler of Riverstone and more like a man emptied out. Silent. Strung out. Finished.

The shop went still. Clippers buzzed in the background, nobody speaking at first.

One of the older OGs broke the silence. "Damn... look at him. That's how the King of Riverstone go out?" A younger Seven shook his head. "Ain't no king left. That boy look like a fiend. Streets gon' clown him forever." "Don't laugh too hard," another warned. "Feds don't stop with one crown. They keep swinging 'til they knock down the whole table."

Damion leaned forward, eyes locked on the screen. He didn't smile. Didn't joke. Just watched as the Feds pushed Calvin into the back of a van, the woman's voice steady as ever. *"Y'all seeing it live. Baymoor about to change."*

The chat rolled across the screen, comments flying:

- *Rusty set him up.*

- *Nah, Catherine and that cop Grayson pulled the trigger.*

- *Committee finished. Sevens next.*

The shop buzzed with voices, some heated, some worried.

Marcus finally set his clippers down, shaking his head. "Whole city gon' talk about this for weeks." Before anyone could answer, the shop door creaked open. Heads turned. Reggie stepped inside, dressed sharp, presence heavy, cutting through the chatter. The livestream was still playing, Calvin's broken face frozen on the screen. Marcus clicked the phone dark and slid it away. The room shifted again, all eyes moving from the dark screen to Reggie, waiting to see what came next.

CHAPTER TWENTY-NINE

The air in Marcus's shop was still heavy from the livestream replay. Calvin's blank, strung-out face in cuffs lingered in everybody's mind, even with the screen dark now. The hum of clippers filled the silence, broken only when the bell over the door jingled again. Three men stepped inside — OGs from the Committee, familiar but cautious. Their presence shifted the room, younger Sevens leaning back in their chairs, eyes narrowing. Marcus didn't flinch. "Y'all need cuts, or y'all need conversation?" The oldest of the three raised his hand, palms open. "We here for words, not smoke."

They gathered near the back, Marcus wiping his clippers, Damion standing from his chair. The tension was thick enough to choke on. "We not blind," the OG began. "Calvin gone. Feds tore the head off the Committee. Now it's a mess — some OGs with us, some YNs wildin'. They talkin' war. Want blood for Tyreek, want to take their shot at y'all. But that ain't us." Another OG nodded. "We came to tell y'all straight: if bullets fly, it ain't from our side. We ain't got no beef with the Sevens. Truth is..." He hesitated, then let it out. "We'd rather stand *with* y'all than against. Ain't no future in dyin' for a war Calvin started and couldn't finish."

The weight of his words sank in. The room was still, younger Sevens watching every move. Damion studied the men, his face unreadable.

One of the younger Committee members with them — barely twenty — added quickly, "Just keep your shooters pointed the other way. We don't want this fight. We just want to breathe."

Marcus leaned back against the counter, eyes sharp. "That sound like a cop out." "It is," the first OG admitted. "But it's also respect. We came to say it man to man, not hide behind no rumor. Sevens ain't our enemy. We want peace. Maybe even unity."

The shop was thick with the weight of history — two crews that had shed blood now standing inches from something different. Before anyone could answer, the bell over the door chimed again. Serenity stepped in. Hair tied up, outfit clean, moving with quiet purpose. All eyes shifted. Marcus smirked, breaking the tension with a laugh. "Boy, you got it goin' on today, huh?" He looked at Damion, shaking his head. "Committee on one side, your woman on the other... you must be the mayor of Baymoor now." The room rippled with low laughter, but Damion's eyes were locked on Serenity.

CHAPTER THIRTY

The shop was still buzzing from the Committee OGs' visit, their words hanging in the air like smoke even after they left. But all of that faded the second Serenity walked in. She didn't greet anyone. Just locked eyes with Damion. "Can we talk?" The way she said it wasn't a question. Marcus raised his brows, smirking. "Told you, boy, you the mayor." But Damion ignored him, rising from his chair. He followed Serenity out into the cool evening, the door swinging shut behind them.

They stood on the sidewalk, the hum of Westview traffic passing by. Serenity crossed her arms, steadying herself before speaking. "This Rico case..." she began. "They tearing Riverstone apart. It don't stop there, Damion. You know Grayson got it out for you. He ain't gon' stop until it's you in cuffs. Or worse." Damion shook his head, jaw tight. "That got nothin' to do with me. I ain't Calvin. I ain't runnin' no Committee operation. Sevens don't move like that." Serenity's eyes burned. "You don't get it, do you? They don't care about facts. Grayson don't need proof. All he need is a reason. And you keep givin' him one, just by bein' who you are."

The heat rose between them, sharp words sparking like flint. Damion took a step closer, voice low, hard. "So what, Ne-Ne? You want me to disappear? Lay down, let him run me over? That ain't me." Serenity's breath trembled. She cut him off, her voice cracking but firm. "You ain't just livin' for yourself no more, Damion." He froze, searching her face. "What you mean by that?"

She held his gaze, no turning back. Her voice dropped to a whisper, but the words landed like thunder.
"I'm pregnant, Damion."

ACKNOWLEDGEMENT

To those who helped shaped this journey:

Support- Tasha Crawfod, Lashonda Brewer, & Demonica Mcfarland. Thank you for standing by me and always encouraging me.

Inspiration- Joe Baker, Boo Baker, and Bill Feezy. Your stories and testimonies has been a driving influence.

In Remembrance:
Auntie Bessie Mae, Auntie Brina, Auntie Maria and
Auntie Wanda
Mauricio Nance, Tyshun Fields, Demario Snell and
Fredrick Carter

ABOUT THE AUTHOR

Danyae Brewer

About the Author
Danyae Brewer is a Mississippi-born author whose storytelling captures the raw emotion, complexity, and power of modern urban life. At just 29 years old, he's building a creative universe that blends street realism with cinematic depth, inspired by series like Power, Snowfall, and The Wire.

Through his debut novel Asia's Agenda, Brewer explores love, loyalty, trauma, and redemption in a world where every choice comes with a cost. His mission is bigger than fiction—he writes to spark what he calls a Gangster's Renaissance, using storytelling to inspire financial, mental, and spiritual growth within the Black community. When he's not writing or working, Danyae enjoys spending time with his two children, Elijah and Elliana, and creating art that challenges, uplifts, and redefines the culture.

Made in the USA
Middletown, DE
24 November 2025

22209539R00076